P9-CCW-530

DISCARDED

The Double Life of Pocahontas

The Double Life of POCAHONTAS

JEAN FRITZ

with illustrations by Ed Young

G. P. PUTNAM'S SONS

NEW YORK

My special thanks to Dr. Frederick Fausz of the
Institute of Early American History and Culture
for his generous and critical assistance.

 Published simultaneously in
Canada by General Publishing Co. Limited, Toronto.
Printed in the United States of America
Design by Nanette Stevenson
First Impression

Library of Congress Cataloging in Publication Data
Fritz, Jean. The double life of Pocahontas.
Bibliography: p. Includes index.
Summary: A biography of the famous American Indian
princess, emphasizing her life-long adulation of John Smith
and the roles she played in two very different cultures.
1. Pocahontas, d. 1617—Juvenile literature.
2. Powhatan Indians—Biography—Juvenile literature.
3. Jamestown (Va.)—History—Juvenile literature.
4. Virginia—History—Colonial period, ca. 1600-1775—
Juvenile literature. [1. Pocahontas, d. 1617.
2. Indians of North America—Biography. 3. Smith, John,
1580-1631. 4. Powhatan, ca. 1550-1618. 5. Jamestown
(Va.)—History. 6. Virginia—History—Colonial period,
ca. 1600-1775] I. Young, Ed, ill. II. Title.
E99.P85P573 1983 975.5'01'0924 [B] [92] 83-9662
ISBN 0-399-21016-4

For Margaret Frith

1

Pocahontas had every reason to be happy. It was the budding time of the year; who would not be happy? The world was new-green, cherry trees were afroth, and strawberries, like sweet red secrets, fattened on the ground. At first birdcall, Pocahontas would run splashing into the river, and along with the others in the village she would wait to greet the Sun as it rose.

Together they would watch the sky turn from gray to pink, to gold. Then suddenly they would shout. There it came! And was it not a wonder that always it returned again and yet again? All the people welcomed it, scattering sacred tobacco into a circle, lifting up their hands and singing to please their god, Okee, in the way their priests had taught them. One must never forget Okee, for it was He who held danger in his hands—lightning, floods, drought, sickness, war.

Indeed, Pocahontas could hardly help but be happy. At eleven, she was the right age for happiness. Still young enough to romp with the children, yet old enough to join the dance of unmarried girls. And how she danced—whirling and stamping and shouting until her breath was whisked into the wind, until she had grown wings like a bird, until she had become sister to the trees, until she was at one with everything that lived and grew. With the world itself, round like a plate under the sky. And in the center of the plate, there was her father, the great Chief Powhatan, seated high, twelve mats under him, raccoon robe around him with tails dangling. And beside him, there was Pocahontas herself, for was she not her father's favorite? Did he not say that Pocahontas was as dear to him as his own life? So of course Pocahontas was happy.

Around the edges of the world plate, Pocahontas knew, were unfriendly tribes. And somewhere on the far, far rim beyond the waters there were strangers from a land she could not picture at all. Sometimes these strangers came to her father's kingdom, coat-wearing men with hair on their faces. The last time, these men had kidnapped a chief's son and killed a chief, but since then the geese had flown north three times and they had not come back. Perhaps they would not come again.

There was no way, of course, for Pocahontas to know that at that very moment three English ships with one hundred and four such coat-wearing men were approaching Chesapeake Bay. No one told these men that the land was taken, that this was Powhatan's kingdom, but even if they had, the English would not have cared. Naked savages, they would have said—they were like herds of deer. How could they legally own land? The world was made for civilized people, for people who wouldn't let the land go to waste, for people who knew the right way to live. In other words, for Christians.

The year, according to the Christian calendar, was 1607, and these Christians were here to stay. They had already named this place Virginia, and they meant to make it theirs. Still mad at themselves for having said No to Christopher Columbus when they might have said Yes and beaten the Spanish to the New World, they were going to make up for lost time. They had their directions from London. They were to find gold. And a shortcut to the other ocean. They were to be friendly to the natives and turn them into

Christians. Finally, they were to provide goods that would make money for England.

They were told to build their houses in straight lines. And when they wrote home, they were to write cheerful letters.

By the time that the English reached Chesapeake Bay (April 26, 1607), however, they had little cheerful to say. After four months of being cooped up on shipboard, the one hundred and four passengers were sick to death of each other. John Smith, a twenty-seven-year-old adventurer, could not abide Master Edward Wingfield (who would be president of the ruling council) with his high and mighty airs. In turn Master Wingfield heartily disliked John Smith, an upstart who acted as if he knew it all. Both men were suspicious of Captain Gabriel Archer, a born troublemaker, and both were impatient with Captain John Ratcliffe, who wanted to go home when the seas became too rough. Poor Robert Hunt, the preacher, tried to keep peace among the passengers, but it was hard, especially since he was seasick so often. John Smith reported that he made "wild vomits into the black night." One of the few men who seemed to command the respect of all was one-armed Captain Christopher Newport, who was in charge of the expedition while at sea. Everyone thought it was lucky that his name was Christopher, like Christopher Columbus.

But once they had landed and started exploring, the spirits of the men rose. What a paradise Virginia was! Raccoons as big as foxes, they reported. Possums like month-old pigs. Vines the size of a man's thigh. Strawberries four times bigger than English strawberries, and oysters thick as stones. Best of all, there were rocks that sparkled. Gold, John Martin said, and since his father was a goldsmith, he should know. And up the river there was a two-mile-long peninsula, a perfect place to settle. They tied their ships up to the trees and called the place Jamestown in honor of their king at home.

There were also natives whom the English called "savages." They encountered them when they first went ashore. After their long trip, the men were so glad to stretch their legs, they stayed until dark, not noticing the five Indians creeping on hands and knees through the tall grass, their bows in their mouths. Then all at once the air was filled with arrows. Captain Archer was shot in both hands; a sailor was wounded.

Then the English fired their guns, and the natives darted back to the woods.

John Smith was the one who seemed to know most about handling the natives. At least he claimed he did. Before joining this expedition, he had fought the Turks in Europe. He'd been captured, made a slave, and had so many narrow escapes that he figured he understood "savages" pretty well. Gentleness was not the way to deal with them, he said. The English should show strength; they should rely on fear, not love, to keep peace. This was only common sense, but John was afraid there wasn't much common sense among these settlers.

The English built a fort on their peninsula, and as they settled down they found there were natives all around them. Many seemed friendly, glad to exchange corn for tiny bells and pretty glass beads. (Pocahontas would love those beads.) When the English clapped their hands over their hearts in the sign of friendship, the natives would lower their bows, give two shouts of welcome, and offer food and pipes of tobacco. Once a chieftain, wearing a crown of bear's hair, played a flute. They even told the

English that, yes, the ocean they were looking for was just ahead. Up the river and beyond the falls.

Yet other Indians were not one bit friendly. Once they killed an English boy and shot an arrow right through President Wingfield's beard. Often they lay in the tall grass outside the English fort, waiting for someone to come through the gate. Not even a dog could run out safely. Once one did and had forty arrows shot into his body.

But all the Indians were curious. Especially Powhatan. What were the strangers doing here? Did they mean to stay? When after two months (on June 22) Captain Newport and two ships sailed back to England for supplies, the Indians were wild with curiosity. Where were the ships going? What did it mean?

Powhatan's brother, Opechancanough, chief of the Pamunkeys, one of Powhatan's most important tribes, sent a messenger to Jamestown.

Where had the ships gone? he wanted to know.

Oh, not far. Just south a little way, the settlers answered.

A few days later Powhatan himself sent messengers. Where were the ships? they asked.

Nearby, they were told.

Perhaps the strangers would leave soon, Powhatan thought. All they had done here was to trade for corn and more corn and still more corn. Perhaps in their country there was no land for growing corn. So when they had enough food, maybe they would go home. In the meantime he might get guns from the strangers. How he marveled at the power of guns! How he loved their thunderclaps! How he longed for guns of his own!

It would be months, however, before either Powhatan or Pocahontas would meet any strangers face to face. In the meantime Pocahontas went about her life as usual in the village of Werowocomoco where she lived, greeting the Sun as it rose, honoring it again as it left the world in the evening.

In Jamestown the settlers held their own ceremonies. Twice a day their preacher, Robert Hunt, read a prayer written especially for the colonists by King James of England. They prayed that the "savages" would be converted to Christianity. How else, they asked themselves, could they get along in the New World?

But as the summer wore on, all the settlers really wanted was to stay alive. The Indians had run out of corn, and, until Captain Newport returned from England with fresh supplies, the settlers had nothing to eat but half a pint of wheat every day and half a pint of wormy barley boiled in water. All they had to drink was water from the river, salty at high tide, slimy at low tide. They quit trying to hunt or fish because whenever they left the fort, arrows came flying out of the tall grass. So it was no wonder that one after another the settlers fell sick and one after another they died.

By the end of the summer fifty men, almost half the colony, had died and the rest were bickering and quarreling with each other. On one thing, however, they agreed: President Wingfield was wicked. They accused him of hoarding food for himself, of liking the Spaniards (England's enemy), of wanting to be a king, and of being an atheist since, as far as anyone could see, he didn't own a Bible. Moreover, he wouldn't work and he didn't know how to get others to work. In all this time none of their houses had been finished and hardly anything had been planted. So Edward Wingfield was removed as president. Captain Ratcliffe was elected in his place, and John Smith was put in charge of what went on outside the fort.

Meanwhile in Powhatan's kingdom the corn had ripened and the people were celebrating their harvest. There were games—football (only the foot was allowed to touch the ball), a stickball game (like lacrosse), contests of racing, catching, leaping. There was feasting and dancing. Bonfires blazed over the country while men, women, and children danced around the fires, shaking rattles and clapping hands. The men sang songs about the brave things they would do now that their work was done.

One of the first things they decided to do was to trade. Who knew what those hungry settlers might be willing to part with now? Perhaps a copper kettle (a prize indeed). Perhaps a sword or two. Perhaps even a gun. So off to Jamestown they went, loaded down with corn, fruit, pumpkin, squash, turkey—everything a hungry man would dream of. The settlers, of course, gobbled up everything that the Indians brought, and in return they gave the Indians beads and bells, some copper, a hatchet or two. But no guns. John Smith said Indians should never be given a chance even to handle a gun.

Along with the food, one of the Indians gave the settlers a piece of advice. Cut down that long grass outside the fort, he said.

Now that there was corn again, John Smith began to make trading trips up the river and to go on explorations. Maybe he'd find gold, maybe that other ocean. Who knew what he might find in this wonderful land? As young as he was, John was well traveled. Not only had he fought in every war he could find, he had walked, ridden, hitchhiked over much of Europe, but no place had ever moved him as this one did. He could not round the bend of a river without feeling excited at the newness, the wildness, the bigness of this world. What luck it was that he was young and that he was here and that he had his whole life to give to it. Wherever he went, he made maps, carefully drawing in the winding course of rivers that had never been drawn before, giving names to places that had never had English names.

In December he and nine other men were on such an expedition when they were surprised by a hunting party of Pamunkey Indians. At the moment John and an Indian guide were walking inland and didn't know that back on the riverbank two Englishmen had been killed. (The rest got away.) John knew nothing of the danger until all at once arrows were flying from all directions. He grabbed his Indian guide, buckled the Indian's arm to his own with a garter, and, using him as a shield, he held the Indian in front of him with one hand and held his pistol with the other.

Slowly the Indians encircled him—two hundred of them—while John fired his pistol, killing two in short order. The most excited person there, of course, was the Indian guide who stood between the arrows and the bullets. He called frantically to the hunters to put away their arrows. This man was a chief, he said; *he was a chief.* Indians did not kill a chief carelessly. Not right away. Not without more authority. So the hunters agreed to lay down their bows if the English chief would give up his gun.

But John Smith wouldn't. Still holding on to his guide, he brandished his pistol as he began backing toward the river. At least he supposed he was going toward the river. Instead he and his guide suddenly fell into a swamp, such a deep "oozy" swamp there was no way to get out without help. Yet how could John Smith get help and still hold on to his gun? Obviously he couldn't. So, much as he hated to, he threw his pistol on the ground and let the Indians pull him to dry land and make him their captive. After that, for weeks he was marched across the country to be displayed to one village after another, to meet chiefs, to be examined by priests. The natives were all interested in the same questions: What were the English doing here? How long would they stay? When would their big chief, the man with one arm, be back? In the end John Smith was taken to Werowocomoco to see Powhatan, who would decide what was to be done with him.

Long before he arrived the people at Werowocomoco knew about him. Pocahontas would have heard about his magic disc with its arrow that swung around and pointed in one direction no matter how it was turned or shaken. She would have learned that this stranger said the world was round. Not round like a plate but round like a ball. Like an apple. Everyone agreed that he was a man with much magic.

What would happen to him? Pocahontas knew her father could have him killed. Piece by piece, perhaps. Or by burning. Pocahontas had watched both ways. But sometimes a captive was adopted into a tribe. First he would be purified in a ceremony that looked as if the captive would be killed, but instead at the last minute he would seem to be saved by a member of the tribe, a woman usually, to whom he would forever be kin.

Pocahontas was present in her father's great longhouse when John Smith arrived, a short, straight-standing man with a furry beard and bright, fearless eyes. He marched past two hundred of Powhatan's bodyguards, all glaring at him, but John Smith showed no fear. Not even before Powhatan himself who sat high on his matted throne—a large, stately figure, every inch a king.

Of course Pocahontas was impressed by this short stranger. Indians always admired courage, and, according to all reports, this man had not only stood up alone to two hundred warriors, he had struck fear into their hearts. Not just by his gun but by himself. By his very boldness. And here he was striding into an enemy stronghold, into her father's court, without the slightest sign that he felt danger. She watched him wash his hands in the water that was brought to him and dry them on feathers as if this was his daily custom. And when Powhatan questioned him, she marveled that he did not flinch and quail as so many prisoners did. No, he spoke out firmly.

Why had the English come? Powhatan wanted to know.

It was all a mistake, John Smith said. They had been fighting their enemy, the Spanish, and had been blown here by a storm.

Why were they staying?

Oh, they were just waiting for Captain Newport to come back. Then they'd go home.

Perhaps Powhatan had already decided what to do with John Smith; perhaps he decided later. In any case, he had guns on his mind. And if he adopted John Smith into the tribe, John would be required to give him gifts. What better gift than guns? A couple of cannon to start off with, maybe. Then, as his mind ran on, Powhatan may have caught the eye of Pocahontas. She looked so interested, eager—well, why not let her be the man's sponsor?

All John Smith knew, however, was that a fire was being lighted. The priests were wailing and calling on their gods as if they were preparing for a sacrifice. Powhatan was conferring with his chiefs. Then he gave an order and John was dragged forward and forced to lay his head on two huge stones. Tall men stood around him with raised clubs, and at any moment John expected to have his brains bashed out.

Suddenly a little girl rushed up to him. She put his head in her arms and begged for his life. Maybe this was prearranged; maybe not. No one can know for sure, but the important thing was: John was saved. The men with the clubs drew back and John was helped to his feet. Of course he was delighted to have his brains intact. And pleased to make the acquaintance of Pocahontas, who had been his savior.

But she was more than that. In her view, she was his sister now. He was her brother, and Powhatan was father to them both. He could live at Werowocomoco, as adopted members of a family often did. He could play games with her, string beads, and make hatchets for her father. They had a special kinship, and if he stayed he would be her countryman.

Did he understand?

Powhatan also wanted to make sure that John Smith understood he'd been adopted into the tribe. To make it seem official, Powhatan and two hundred of his warriors painted themselves black and descended on John Smith one night. Powhatan explained that John Smith was not only Powhatan's adopted son, he was a chief. Like all his chiefs, he would be expected to give Powhatan gifts. What Powhatan wanted right now were two thunder weapons (cannon) and a millstone for grinding corn. Rawhunt (Powhatan's lieutenant) and twelve guards would go to Jamestown with John Smith to bring back the gifts.

John Smith agreed. Pocahontas would not have let him go without saying goodbye, and John would have made a formal farewell to Powhatan, whom he gladly called "father."

Once at the settlement, John showed Rawhunt the millstone. Rawhunt's body was deformed so that he did not expect to move the millstone himself, but none of the twelve guards could move it, either.

Well, there were the cannon, John Smith pointed out. Rawhunt knew how much Powhatan was counting on those cannon, so he urged the guards to try hard, to use every muscle. But it was no use. Each cannon weighed between 3,000 and 4,500 pounds.

It was too bad, John said, that the Indians couldn't take the cannon home. He'd give them other gifts instead. He gathered up some trinkets, bells, baubles of glass and copper.

But Powhatan was expecting thunder.

No thunder, John said.

So the Indians went home, disgruntled, while John Smith, a free man again after six weeks of captivity, walked happily into Jamestown to report to the council on his narrow escape.

He saw at once that Gabriel Archer had taken his place on the council. He also saw that Archer and Ratcliffe, obviously into some mischief or other, were upset to have him back. Indeed, as he soon found out, he was not a free man, after all.

He was under arrest, Archer told him.

Arrest! For what?

Murder.

Whose murder?

The murder of those two men in his party who had been killed by the Indians. He had been responsible for them, hadn't he? He had *let* them get killed. So he was guilty.

Ratcliffe, who always agreed with Archer, chimed in. Captain Smith knew what the Bible said, didn't he? "An eye for an eye." So, as president of the council, Ratcliffe sentenced John Smith to death. He would be executed the next morning.

Put under guard, John Smith fumed. To have escaped the Indians, only to be put to death by his own people! He had always boasted that he was a lucky fellow, but where was his luck now?

Actually, luck was at that very moment gliding toward him up the river. That same evening, just in the nick of time, Captain Newport arrived back from England. He tied his ship up at Jamestown, and as soon as he heard the news he persuaded the council members to set John Smith free and to remove Captain Archer from the council.

Of course the natives had seen Captain Newport arrive. Like the others, Pocahontas would have wondered. Did this mean the strangers would leave now? John Smith too? In a few days they had more news. Captain Newport had brought eighty new settlers with him. It looked as if they meant to stay.

Powhatan would have felt one way about this. Pocahontas might have felt another.

Captain Newport was returning with strict orders from the London Company, which was paying for the Jamestown project. Naturally the men who had put their money into the London Company wanted to get rich as fast as possible. When they heard that Newport had brought back rocks that John Martin, the goldsmith's son, claimed were gold, they were delighted. But when the rocks were tested and turned out not to have one speck of gold in them, the London men said John Martin was a cheat. On his next trip Captain Newport better bring back *real* gold, they said. And good news too. By this time the colony should be in good working order and the Indians should have become obedient and friendly.

But of course, as Captain Newport could see, all the settlers had done in his absence was to fight among themselves. And die. There were only thirty-eight survivors, all of them ravenous for the good English food he'd brought with him. Cheese, pork, beef, butter. And drink. Real drink, not dirty river water. Now they'd settle down and start over.

They didn't know that they'd have to start from scratch. Five days after Newport's arrival, a fire broke out in Jamestown. From thatched roof to thatched roof the flames leaped until all but three small buildings had burned down. Reverend Hunt wasn't able to save a single book from his precious library. The church was destroyed and the storehouse which contained much of the food that Captain Newport had brought with him.

But they didn't go hungry. As soon as Powhatan heard what had happened, he began sending food to Jamestown. Every four or five days it was delivered, and along with the food and the food-carriers came Pocahontas, a special ambassador from her father to John Smith and Captain Newport.

Pocahontas had two worlds now, and she was doubly happy, traveling back and forth from her own familiar world ruled by her father to the strange new world of John Smith. She placed great importance on her kinship to John—more perhaps than her people commonly did, but then she was younger than sponsors generally were, and, as anyone could see, John Smith was not a common kind of man. So it was not surprising that she felt a special belongingness. It was as if they were forever bound together as members of each other's worlds. Nor was it surprising that John humored her, although he himself did not take the kinship seriously. What harm was there in being the favorite of the king's favorite daughter?

In John's world, Pocahontas worked off her high spirits by challenging two or three boys in the settlement to contests of leaping and running. In turn, the boys taught her how to turn cartwheels, which became a favorite sport of hers. In follow-the-leader fashion she'd lead the boys and away they'd go, hand over hand, feet flying. Much of the time, however, she spent with John Smith, watching him work, coaxing him to play, exchanging words—English for Indian, Indian for English. John, who used every opportunity to learn the language, had a book in which he wrote down Indian words, and perhaps, as their speaking together improved, Pocahontas was able to explain that her name meant "lively" or "frolicsome." Even to her adopted brother, however, she would not have confessed her real name, Matoaka (sometimes translated "Little Snow Feather") because that was a secret between her and her clan. To speak one's real name aloud was like opening a door to evil spirits, and Pocahontas was far too pleased with her life right now to take any chance with evil spirits.

Once John Smith wrote down a long sentence that he could use when he wanted to send Pocahontas a message: *"Kekaten Pokahontas patiaquagh niugh tanks manotyens mawokick rawrenock audawgh."*

Beside the Indian words, John wrote the English translation: "Bid Pocahontas bring hither two little Baskets and I will give her white Beads to make her a Chaine."

He would not have bothered to learn such a long sentence unless he expected to use it more than once. And indeed on every trip to Jamestown Pocahontas added to her store of presents from John. On her return home, she would show off her treasures and perhaps share them with her half sisters. (She had many, for her father, as the chief, had many wives.) Sometimes she taught her sisters and friends English phrases she had learned, not always from John Smith but from the boys she played with as well. There was one phrase which always made the English boys laugh: "Love you not me?" Indeed, she was asked to say the phrase so often that when she went home she taught it to her friends. "Love you not me? Love you not me?" They would all laugh and repeat it over and over. "Love you not me?"

The Indians had become so friendly now that Captain Newport marveled, and in turn he became friendly with them. Too friendly, John Smith said. Captain Newport couldn't see that in spite of the gifts, the friendship was shaky. The only way to handle the natives, as John had said again and again, was to be firm, to stay on guard, and keep the upper hand.

But Captain Newport was not firm and he didn't stay on guard. He let his sailors trade with the Indians on any terms they wanted. The Indians hardly had to bargain at all. Sure, the sailors said, they could have copper for a small amount of corn. It didn't matter to them. They'd be going home soon.

John Smith just wished they'd go. The longer they stayed, the more food they ate, the more beer they drank, and the less there was for the settlers. The longer they stayed, the more the corn would cost.

At the end of February Captain Newport insisted that John take him to meet Powhatan. To play safe, John took thirty or forty armed men to act as bodyguards. At Werowocomoco he and some of his men went ahead to make sure that everything was peaceful.

Certainly the town appeared peaceful. As a sign of welcome Powhatan had ordered forty or fifty platters of bread to be placed on the ground before his longhouse, and when John appeared the Indians gave him two great shouts of greeting. Inside the longhouse Powhatan was seated on his mats, smiling, surrounded by forty of his wives painted and bejeweled for the occasion. At the sight of John, Powhatan exclaimed again and again how happy he was. He moved over to make a place for John to sit beside him.

Of course John had brought gifts, and of course Powhatan was eager to see what they were. There were three gifts.

A suit of red woolen cloth.

A high "sugarloaf" hat like the one King James wore (when he wasn't wearing his crown).

And a white greyhound dog. Powhatan loved dogs, and since he had never seen one like this he made a great fuss over it.

But where, he asked, were the cannon he'd been promised?

Rawhunt had refused them, John Smith replied.

Powhatan laughed. He understood very well the trick that John had played on him. The next time John should find lighter cannon, he said. Then he asked about the Englishmen outside. Why were they there? Let them be brought in.

John had told his bodyguard to come in two at a time so that the longhouse would never be left unprotected.

Powhatan watched the guns file in with the soldiers holding on to them. Two by two the guns came. So many of them. The men should put their guns on the ground, Powhatan said, to show respect.

Only enemies asked them to do this, Smith replied. Not friends.

There is no mention of Pocahontas in John Smith's account of this visit, but surely she was there, smiling to see how John and her father played a kind of game with each other. Her father would make a demand and John would counter. Usually John won, but Powhatan did not get angry, for both understood the rules of the game.

When Captain Newport arrived, Powhatan began the same game. He asked Newport why his men were armed. Weren't they all friends?

Of course they were friends, Newport replied, and he ordered the entire bodyguard to retreat to the river. He didn't understand the game at all. When trading began, Captain Newport let Powhatan win every time. For a small amount of corn, he gave away twelve big copper kettles. Indeed, all Powhatan had to do was point to a hatchet and the hatchet was his.

Standing on the sidelines, John Smith was growing huffier and huffier. How could he ever expect fair trade again? John was the one who would have to see that the settlement was fed, not Newport. And look what he was doing! In desperation John brought out some blue beads, a kind that the natives had not seen. When Powhatan showed interest, Smith paid little attention. These beads? He didn't have many of these, he said, and he really didn't care to part with them. These were a special blue, having taken their color from the sky. Only very important kings could afford to wear them. The more John Smith talked about the beads, the more Powhatan wanted them. In the end, John was able to wangle over two hundred bushels of corn for a few pounds of the cheap glass beads. He made up for Newport's bungling, but he didn't get rid of Newport.

Newport still had to find gold. This time John Martin, who didn't like being called a cheat, was sure that he'd found the real thing. Indeed, he got the men in the settlement so excited that they would do nothing but dig for gold. "There was no talk, no hope, no work," one settler reported, "but dig gold, refine gold, load gold." John Smith didn't even believe it was gold, but Captain Newport wouldn't sail until he had filled his ship with what John called "Martin's gilded dirt."

On April 10, 1608, Captain Newport finally decided he had enough and he left for England. Along with him went Master Wingfield, Captain Archer, and Namontack, a servant boy of Powhatan's who was learning English and was to report on what he saw. Newport also took two tortoises and two ears of corn, for King James loved to get curiosities from the New World. (Already he had two crocodiles and a wild boar which Newport had brought from a trip to the West Indies.)

Just before Newport sailed, Powhatan sent him a gift of twenty wild turkeys and asked for twenty swords in return. Without hesitation Newport handed over the swords and took the turkeys.

After Newport sailed, Powhatan sent twenty turkeys to John Smith and in the same way asked for twenty swords. John replied with a thundering No. Beads and bells, yes. A copper kettle, maybe. But swords? Never.

The Indians, however, were used to getting what they wanted now. If they couldn't do it one way, they'd do it another. They'd steal—swords, if possible; hatchets, if they were handy. They even tried to grab weapons out of the hands of settlers, but when they attempted to surround John Smith in a cornfield they went too far. Not only did Smith succeed in getting safely back to Jamestown, he managed to take seven Indian captives with him.

Powhatan tried to get the captives released. First one way, then another. Finally he sent Pocahontas to Jamestown, along with Rawhunt, some relatives of the captured Indians, and the gift of a deer. But Pocahontas was not to beg, Powhatan warned her. She was the daughter of a king. She should simply present John Smith with the deer and assure him of Powhatan's love. Let Rawhunt and the relatives do the begging.

So Pocahontas put aside her coaxing, frolicsome ways. She stood straight and proud as a princess, and in the end John Smith and the ruling council agreed that for her sake they would let the prisoners go. But first the prisoners must attend a church service. They had been required to do this every day they'd been in Jamestown, and it is possible that Pocahontas, Rawhunt, and the visiting relatives went, too.

This time those Englishmen who owned armor wore it to church as if they wished to impress the natives that their god was the god of war power. Perhaps the natives were awed, as the English intended them to be, at the sight of metal-suited men clanking up and down on their knees. Yet if Pocahontas was there, she must have wondered at this strange English god who wanted no joy, no dancing, no shouting. Their priest did not even raise a sweat with his talking; indeed, half the time he talked with his eyes closed. Surely if Pocahontas was there, she was glad to get out into the sunshine again. She may even have turned a cartwheel before seeking out John Smith, who as usual was ready to make her happy with presents.

With the return of the captives, Powhatan's people kept more to themselves. As a favorite princess, Pocahontas would probably not have had to help with the planting or do as much work as the other girls her age did, but she would have helped care for the younger children. She may have woven baskets, or sewn skins together for her skirts, decorated them with beads, gathered flowers for her hair. Pocahontas would not have visited John Smith's world this summer, for John was not there. Yet to know her story one must follow John too.

And he was off exploring with a party of fourteen men. He didn't find either the Pacific Ocean or a gold mine, but he did travel three thousand miles, throughout Chesapeake Bay, up the Potomac River, nosing into inlets, following one crooked creek after another. He added new names on his map and drew new rivers and streams. He dug up some ore that might be silver. He saw animals—otters, beavers, martins, minks whose fur would certainly bring money in England.

And fish! He'd never seen so many fish. They were packed so thick in one place that the barge had to push through them. They looked like good eating fish too, but the men had no nets with them. John Smith grabbed a frying pan and tried to scoop some up in it, but, as one explorer said, "we found it a bad instrument to catch fish with." Then John began spearing fish with his sword. This worked better.

He would have done even better, however, if he'd left the fish alone. He was pulling a flat fish with a long tail off his spear when suddenly the fish, a stingray, flipped its tail around and plunged it deep into John's wrist. The poison in the sting was so powerful that within a few hours John's hand, arm, and shoulder were so swollen and he was in such pain that no one thought he would live. Carried ashore, he showed his friends the spot where he wanted to be buried and told them to start digging. It was maddening, of course, that one fish could do what the Indians and the Turks (and even Ratcliffe and Archer) had failed to do.

But, as he always said, John Smith was a lucky fellow. In the end the fish failed, too. By night the swelling was down; John Smith ate the stingray for supper, named the land Sting Ray Isle (known today as Stingray Point), and if he used the grave at all it was only to bury fishbones.

John returned from his explorations on September 7 (1608) and as usual found trouble in Jamestown. This time President Ratcliffe had been acting up. Taking food out of the storehouse so he could eat in style. Ordering the settlers to build him a palace in the woods. Acting like a king. Finally the council had arrested him for mutiny, and on

September 10 John Smith was elected the new president.

At last John had a chance to prove what a little common sense could do for the settlement. He had plenty of ideas. No more shirking, for instance. The town still waited for repairs while men bowled in the streets. And no swearing. Bad language had become such a commonplace that a man couldn't even stub his toe without swearing. But a man might think twice, John figured, if a pitcher of water was poured down his sleeve every time he swore. With half a chance, John thought, he'd turn Jamestown into a proper, businesslike settlement yet.

But before John Smith had his chance, Captain Newport came sailing up the river with seventy new settlers—two of them women, the first to come. Newport also had instructions from London which, he said, he'd been given the authority to carry out. John read the instructions. Not one of them made sense.

In the first place, the settlers were told to travel beyond the falls in the James River, where the ocean was supposed to be, and where there might also be gold. (John Martin's gold hadn't been real this time either.) The London Company had sent a barge, knocked down into five parts so it could be carried over the mountains, around the falls, and assembled on the other side. A huge, awkward, heavy thing. John said the only way anyone could carry it was to burn it and carry the ashes in a bag.

The London Company also sent a group of eight Dutchmen and Poles to get the settlers started manufacturing glass and making pitch and tar. But the settlers didn't even have food for the winter, John pointed out, and Newport had brought no supplies this time. And London was talking about glass and tar!

Furthermore, the London Company wanted Powhatan

to be crowned in a ceremony that would make him a subject ruler under King James. Loyal and obedient. For the ceremony they sent Powhatan a huge bed, a basin and ewer, a scarlet coat, and a copper crown.

The English were, of course, doing exactly what Powhatan had already tried to do when he adopted John Smith and made him a chief. It hadn't worked with John Smith, and it wouldn't work with Powhatan. He'd just think, John predicted, that if he could get all these gifts for nothing, what was to keep him from asking for more and more? The settlers didn't have time to waste on such a silly idea, John said. They couldn't even carry that big bed twelve miles overland to Werowocomoco. They'd have to take it by barge up the river, an eighty-mile trip.

Well, instructions were instructions, Captain Newport insisted.

John could see that it was no use to argue. If only Powhatan would come to Jamestown to be crowned! Then let *him* figure out how to get his bed back home.

With four companions and the returning Namontack, John Smith went to Werowocomoco to invite Powhatan to Jamestown for his coronation. But when John got there, Powhatan wasn't home. Pocahontas said her father was only a short distance away and she'd send messengers to get him. Meanwhile she was overjoyed to have John in her world. How she'd entertain him and his friends! And feast them. She'd gather her sisters and friends together to dance for them. She would let John see how enthusiastically her people worshiped their god, how they painted themselves and sang for His pleasure, how they opened their hearts and tired out their bodies for His sake.

Pocahontas ordered wood to be piled on the embers of the sacred fire which was always kept aglow. She had mats placed on the ground for the five Englishmen. Then she and thirty of her friends ran into the woods to prepare for the ceremony. John did not know what to expect, but he had never imagined that thirty girls could make what he called "such hellish shouts and cries." Nor had he dreamed the girls would come out armed—some with bows, some arrows, some swords, some clubs. All had their bodies painted; all wore horns attached to their heads. They did not look or sound like a friendly group, but when John jumped to his feet Pocahontas stopped the dance. With one hand on her heart, the other raised high to call on the Sun to be her witness, she promised that the English would not be harmed. John sat down, and for the next hour he watched the girls dance and sing around the fire, sometimes in such a frenzy of emotion that they seemed to him fiendish. He called the performance an "antic," by which he meant it was a kind of freak show. But, for Pocahontas, it must have been an ecstasy. With John there, surely her spirit soared into the sky, beyond the blue even.

At the end of the dance the girls returned to the woods, took off their horns, and ran back to see how John had enjoyed the performance. Skipping and bobbing around him, they giggled. "Love you not me?" they asked. "Love you not me?"

The next day Powhatan arrived. Like all those in her tribe, Pocahontas would have known how her father's resentment at the English was growing. With Newport's arrival, there was a total of two hundred settlers now—all with guns, all hungry for Indian corn, all expecting Powhatan to bow to their wishes. It was not only that they didn't seem to care that he was king of this land; it was as if Powhatan didn't even have the right to be a king since he wasn't English. So when John Smith invited him to Jamestown to receive presents from King James, Powhatan bristled. He wasn't going to bite on that bait, he said.

"If your king has sent me presents," he replied, "I also am a king and this is my land. . . . Your father [Captain Newport] is to come to me, not I to him, nor yet to your fort."

So they had to take the bed and the crown and the other gifts the long way around by water. Captain Newport insisted that they be accompanied by one hundred and twenty men. He took seventy with him by river; John Smith took fifty by land. When they had all gathered at Werowocomoco, Powhatan took his place on his throne and waited. By this time he would have heard from Namontack about what kind of place England was: stone towers, tall houses with floors on top of floors, long bridges, chariots to carry people around. It was more than Powhatan could imagine or wanted to imagine. He was glum.

Even the trumpet which announced Newport must have been an irritation in his present mood. Powhatan went through the motions that were expected of him, however, receiving the bed, the ewer, the jug, the finger rings sent by an English nobleman, but when it came to the scarlet coat, he balked. Captain Newport wanted him to put it on then and there. Why? Was there some kind of bad magic in it? Namontack told him it was safe to put it on, so he did, but he wasn't happy about it.

But when he was told to kneel so the crown could be put on his head, Powhatan absolutely refused. Even though Namontack said that kneeling was just part of the English custom, he wouldn't do it. He knew the English went on their knees when they talked to their god, and he wouldn't be tricked into doing anything he didn't understand. Finally one of the men pushed down on his shoulders so that in spite of himself Powhatan stooped slightly. Quickly Captain Newport clapped the copper crown on Powhatan's bent head. Outside the longhouse the English fired guns to mark the occasion, but Powhatan was annoyed by all the fuss. He had always been a king; he didn't need the English to make him one again.

Of course he knew that he was expected to give gifts in return for the crown that he didn't want and the coat that he didn't trust. So in an offhand way he handed Newport the deerskin mantle he'd been wearing. He tossed in a pair of his old moccasins and ordered a measly seven bushels of corn to be presented to the English. It was just as John Smith had said: Powhatan would become prouder and stingier; but in fact the coronation probably had little to do with his change of attitude. Crown or no crown, Powhatan had just had enough of the English who could build stone towers and make guns but couldn't even feed themselves. After the English left, Powhatan told his people they were not to trade with them anymore. He told Pocahontas she was not to visit Jamestown; her friendship with John Smith was over. The English were their enemies.

Pocahontas understood that there was nothing more important to her people than loyalty to the tribe. Had she not felt that closeness at every sunrise and every sunset? Had she not celebrated that closeness every time she danced? Yet it was her father who had made John Smith her brother, and how could she order him out of her mind? How could she pretend that John was her enemy?

Yet John did become an enemy to her people. No matter what he had to do, he was going to see that the English settlement survived. If he couldn't get corn by trade, he'd fight for it. He'd burn down houses, if that's what he had to do. He'd destroy what the Indians valued most, their canoes whittled and carved out of tree trunks with such effort, such care. But he *would* feed his people.

Captain Newport was unhappy about all the clashes, and when he went back to London in December he reported that *he* certainly had been friendly to the natives. He described the nice coronation he'd given Powhatan. Indeed, he'd carried out all his instructions, although he admitted there was not much to show for it. Only a few samples of glass and pitch and tar. But no gold. No sign of an ocean, although he'd gone around the falls as he'd been told to, except he hadn't bothered with the barge.

In addition, Newport delivered John Smith's map and a blistering letter from John which blamed the London Company for Jamestown's troubles. How could people in London know, John asked, what instructions to give a country they'd never seen? And how could they expect the kind of men they'd been sending to Jamestown to succeed at anything? The Company kept sending gentlemen who would not work, laborers without skills, runaways and condemned men. "The scumme of the world," John called them. And troublemakers like Ratcliffe (who was returning now with Newport) and Archer (who had already returned). Never let these two return to Jamestown, he wrote.

Back in Jamestown, however, John had made some of the improvements he had had planned. Just as he had predicted, all it took was a pitcher of cold water poured down the sleeve to discourage a man from using bad language. And with his encouragement, there was more attention to business. But it was hard for men to work when they were hungry, and because there was so little trade they were hungry most of the time. So, in January of 1609, when Powhatan suddenly sent John an invitation to visit and the promise of a boatload of corn, John quickly accepted. In return, of course, Powhatan made demands: an English house, a grindstone, copper and beads, fifty swords, some guns, a rooster and a hen.

John did send two Dutchmen and two Englishmen ahead to start building a house, but he was not giving in to all of Powhatan's demands. When he and forty-seven guards arrived at Werowocomoco two weeks later, he had copper and beads with him, probably a rooster and a hen, possibly a grindstone, but certainly no swords or guns.

As it turned out, sending the men ahead to build the house had been a mistake. By the time John arrived, the Dutchmen had decided that life under Powhatan was better than life under John Smith. They decided to stay with Powhatan and promised to get him guns from the settlement. Furthermore, they told him that if he wanted to get rid of the English he should first get rid of John Smith.

This time when John Smith arrived, there were no shouts of greeting for him. No platters of bread to welcome him. Powhatan received him coldly.

What was John Smith doing here? he asked. He hadn't been sent for.

Not sent for? John pointed to the messengers who had come to Jamestown. How could he be so forgetful?

Powhatan laughed, but he was not going to be tricked into easy dealings. If there was any trading to be done, Powhatan said, John Smith should understand that he was not interested in anything but swords and guns.

"I told you long ago," John replied, "I had none to spare."

But Captain Newport had given him swords, Powhatan said. He had put away his guns when asked. Why couldn't John do the same? After all, Powhatan was John's father. As his son and chief, John should do what his father wanted.

John wished no further misunderstanding. "Powhatan," he said, "you must know . . . I honor but one king, and I live here not as your subject but as your friend."

No, not as a friend, Powhatan replied. "Captain Smith, many do inform me," he said, "your coming hither is not for trade, but to invade my people, and possess my country."

All the time that Powhatan had been talking, his warriors had been secretly gathering around his house, and now Powhatan made an excuse to leave the building. With his wives and children, Powhatan ran away, leaving behind several women to entertain John and keep him from becoming suspicious.

But after a while John did become suspicious. He had only eighteen men on shore, who of course were far outnumbered by the natives, but, as it turned out, John didn't need his men. He surprised the warriors who were secretly trying to block his exit, fired his pistol into the group, and at his first shot they all fled.

Pocahontas was one of the children whom Powhatan took with him on his flight. She would have seen the frightened warriors streaking into the woods to tell her father that his plot had failed. She would have watched her father try to smooth things over by sending John a pearl bracelet and chain and an apology for his absence. She also knew that there was already a new plot for doing away with John Smith.

She wanted to warn John, but how could she? Yet when evening came, Pocahontas could not help herself. When no one was looking, she slipped away from her family and ran through the woods until she came to the place where the English were staying. She waited for a chance to speak to John alone.

Go, she begged him. Go quickly. Her words must have tumbled over each other, so great was her haste, so deep her worry. Her father's men were going to try to kill John, she told him. With his own weapons if they could. If not, some other way. Later they would send him food, she said. He should be careful, oh, he should be very careful, for the food might be poisoned.

John told her he would be careful, and he thanked her for coming. He wished he had some presents for her. Now of all times he would have liked to give her something pretty.

But Pocahontas had not come for presents. Tears streaming down her face, she said she didn't want them and couldn't take them if she did. If her father saw that she had presents, he would know what she had done and he would kill her. Quickly Pocahontas turned and ran back through the woods.

An hour later a procession of eight Indians brought the Englishmen huge platters of food, but John made the Indians taste every dish before he and his friends would take even a bite. All night John stayed on guard; all night the Indians looked for a chance to surprise him, but that chance never came. The next morning he left Werowocomoco, but before returning to Jamestown he went in search of corn.

Wherever he went, however, the Indians tried to kill him. On his visit to Powhatan's brother, Opechancanough, warriors tried to lure John outside where they lay in ambush. But John was warned, and in sudden fury he put his pistol on Opechancanough's chest and grabbed him by the lock of hair which, like a bird's crest, he wore in the

Indian style on top of his head. Terrified, Opechancanough and all his warriors surrendered their weapons. A man who could so brazenly insult a chief in the midst of his own people must have no fear for his life, the Indians reasoned. He must have secret magic. Yet later, when they found John taking a nap, they were ready to try again, but John woke up, snatched his sword, and the warriors decided it was no use.

Indeed, there seemed to be no way to get rid of the man. The Indians tried to trap John on his way back to Jamestown, but they didn't succeed. They tried to poison him, but he threw up the poison. The rumor spread: John had secret magic and couldn't be killed. Pocahontas must have heard the rumor. Perhaps she believed; perhaps she only hoped.

When John returned to Jamestown, he found himself suddenly in sole charge of the settlement, the only surviving member of the council. In his absence all the other members had been drowned when their skiff had turned over, which meant that John's word was the law. He had brought back corn and deer suet, so that there was enough food in the storehouse to last until harvest if they were careful. And they would be careful. From now on, John said, no one would eat who didn't work.

For three months the settlers did work and they did eat. Then it wasn't the Indians who stopped them from eating. It was rats! English rats. (There was no such thing as an American rat.) They had come off English ships, settled down, multiplied, and invaded the storehouse. They had eaten all the corn that the English had been counting on. And it was only April.

What were they to do? the settlers asked. Starve again?

No, John Smith said. They were going to divide into

small groups and live off the land, just the way the Indians did when they ran short of food. Some would go down the river where there were plenty of oysters, some to Point Comfort where the fishing was good, some up river near the falls, and some would stay with friendly Indians. The settlers didn't have much faith in the scheme, but they did eat, just as John had said they would.

In August they were still surviving when a fleet of English ships came sailing up the river. The settlers ran to the riverbank.

What news?

Three hundred new settlers, they were told. And a new governor appointed by the king. Lord De La Warre. He was still in England; he wouldn't be able to come until later.

A new charter too. New rules for governing the colony.

The ships tied up, and the newcomers tumbled off the ships. The most conspicuous passenger, however, was no newcomer. Captain Gabriel Archer was back and would have enjoyed telling John the rest of the news.

John Smith was out of a job. The colony was going to be run differently now.

Where was the new charter? John asked.

Well, it was on Captain Newport's flagship, but it wasn't here yet. There had been a storm at sea, and some of the ships had been blown off course.

Who was the deputy governor, John asked—the man in charge until the governor came?

Sir Thomas Gates. He was on the flagship, too.

And the man next in command after Gates?

Sir George Somers. Also on the flagship.

In that case, John declared, he was still in charge. His term as president did not run out until September 10, and unless the flagship arrived before then he would remain president until the end of his term.

Stubbornly John went about his work. Day after day went by, but still no flagship appeared. But four other ships came in and Captain John Ratcliffe was on one of them.

Both Archer and Ratcliffe back! How could there be anything but trouble ahead? Perhaps to get away from town, John decided to go upriver to check on the settlement there, but, as it turned out, this trip was a disaster, too. The settlers upriver were mad at him, the Indians were mad at the settlers, and the place was in danger of flooding. John did what he could and then turned back toward Jamestown.

He was tired, not only tired in his body but tired of people. Of their mutinies, their complaints, their difficulties among themselves, their everlasting unreasonableness. Indeed, it was easier to deal with the Indians than with his own people. On his return trip he lay down on the bottom of his boat to take a nap. As usual the bag in which he kept his gunpowder hung from his waist, lying on his hip. Suddenly a spark, perhaps from someone's pipe, lighted on the bag and it burst into flames. John jumped into the water, but the fire had already burned the flesh off a ten-inch square of his body. He was so severely burned he had to be saved from drowning, and at Jamestown he had to be carried ashore.

As painful as his wound was, however, John Smith was conscious and wanted the news.

No, the flagship had not arrived, he was told. Everyone had decided that it must have sunk, so the settlers had formed a government of their own. Archer and Ratcliffe, of course, had prominent places in the government. John Smith had none.

Well, what could he do? John asked himself. How could he fight these old enemies again? Stripped of his authority, what good was he? What good was he anyway with a wound which kept him on his back and which would take weeks to heal?

Then Ratcliffe hired a man to shoot John in his sleep. The man lost his nerve at the last minute, but John didn't care to test his luck further. He asked to be carried on board one of the returning ships. He was not going to quit the New World. After three years in Virginia, he loved the New World too much to quit it, but he was going to take a rest from it. A few days later he was bound for London.

Of course, the Indians noticed that John Smith was no longer around. Where was he? they asked.

He was dead, the settlers said. Dead and buried.

When Powhatan heard the news, he shook his head. Maybe he was dead; maybe not. The English often lied.

But Pocahontas believed. John Smith loved her land too much to leave it. Moreover, he was too brave to have been frightened off by anything or anyone.

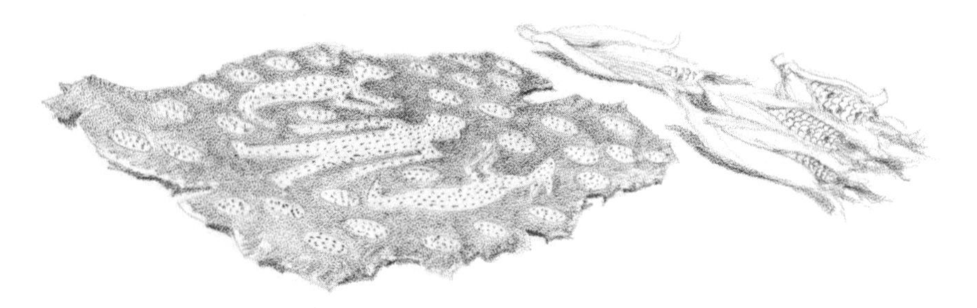

3

As soon as the Indians had made sure that John Smith was out of the way, they descended on Jamestown. No Captain Smith to stop them now! Nothing to be afraid of! They'd get rid of the whole colony. Starve the settlers out. Kill their hogs. Murder anyone caught outside the fort. Steal their guns. Outside the fort day and night, rain or shine, through the fall, winter, and spring, the natives lay in ambush, waiting. *"Yah ha ha Tewittaw Tewittaw,"* they sang whenever they saw an Englishman, whenever they thought the English could hear them, whenever they killed one. It was a taunting song they had made up. *"Yah ha ha."* Every death, they sang, gave them new weapons. *"Yah ha ha Tewittaw Tewittaw."* Each death, another gun! And the settlers, wrangling among themselves, seemed helpless without John Smith to tell them what to do and make them do it. Danger, which often brings out the best in people, brought out the worst in them.

This year became known as the Starving Time. Imprisoned inside their fort, the settlers suffered more hunger, more sickness than they ever had. More people died. (Captain Archer was one of them.) And more were killed. Once forty men, lured up the river by a promise of corn, allowed themselves to become separated from each other, and all were killed. Ratcliffe was tied to a tree and slowly tortured to death.

By the end of the winter, the settlers had eaten what few horses they had (including their hides), all their dogs, and every mouse and rat that they could catch. Some settlers ran away to live with any Indians who would take them;

some begged Indians to take their swords and guns in exchange for even a few grains of corn. One man secretly roasted his dead wife and was hanged for it. Out of a population of five hundred, in the spring of 1610 only sixty men, women, and children were left.

Powhatan, who had moved to a village farther away from the English than Werowocomoco, followed the news closely. He was over seventy years old now, and after a lifetime of fighting he was tired. In his last interview with John Smith he had spoken of his longing for peace. "Think you I am so simple," he had said according to John's account, "not to know it is better to eate good meate, lye well, and sleepe quietly with my women and children, laugh and be merry . . . , than to be so hunted by you that I can neither rest, eate, nor sleepe; but my tyred men must watch, and if a twig but breake, everyone cryeth, there commeth Captain Smith."

Now that the Jamestown colony was all but wiped out, Powhatan looked forward to quiet days. Soon, soon the land would be his again and life would walk in time with the seasons. Meanwhile Powhatan took pleasure in the guns he had collected during the last year. He didn't know how to use them, but that didn't matter. He *owned* them. All that secret power. It was enough simply to look at the guns, to handle them, to pick them up and put them down. Every one of them his.

Of course Pocahontas too longed for peace. Several times she had helped John's countrymen escape from her father's warriors, but it was hard being pulled from one loyalty to another. Now, with John gone, she tried to put his world completely behind her. She made frequent trips to the Potomac country, which was as far as she could get from Jamestown and still be in friendly territory. In the spring of

1610 Pocahontas was fourteen, old enough to marry, and this is what she did. Nothing is known of her Indian husband except his name—Captain Kocoum. Perhaps Powhatan arranged the marriage; perhaps Pocahontas chose Kocoum herself—out of love or out of need, simply to help her forget. Grieving as she must have for John Smith, she may have found it hard to feel the familiar oneness of her old world. In any case, she understood that John's settlement could not last much longer. Once the English were gone, surely it would be as if they had never been there; even the trees would feel the difference.

What no one in Virginia knew, however, was that Captain Newport's flagship had not sunk ten months before as everyone had supposed. Instead, it had been swept onto one of the Bermuda islands, and although the ship itself had been destroyed, all one hundred and fifty passengers had managed to get ashore safely. And there they had been ever since, living off the fruit of the island, off wild hogs and tortoises, off fish and birds. They built themselves cabins and thatched them with palmetto leaves. And they built two large boats, using oak planks from the wrecked ships and timber from cedar trees which they cut. On May 10, 1610, they climbed into the boats and set sail for Jamestown.

On May 23 they arrived, expecting to move into a well-ordered colony, but, of course, as one passenger said, everything was "contrary to our expectations." The place was a shambles; the survivors barely surviving. Governor Gates went straight to the church and had the bell rung to call everyone together. Those who could still walk joined the newcomers for a service in which they prayed to be saved. They knew they couldn't save themselves. The newcomers had only a few days' supply of food, the settlers none. Even among the Indians there was not enough food to fight for. This was planting time, not harvest time.

For two weeks Governor Gates tried to find a way to keep the colony going, but in the end he gave up. If they didn't all want to starve together, he said, there was nothing to do but to abandon Jamestown and go back to England.

So on the seventh of June Governor Gates ordered that drums be beaten while the settlers boarded their boats. They had already buried their cannon, and the men who owned armor had buried it as well. Perhaps some believed that they would come back, but some were so glad to be done with Jamestown, they wanted to burn it to the ground before they left. Nothing would suit them better than to sail down the river, watching the flames devour the place that had proved such a curse to them. After all, why not? As soon as they had left, the Indians would take over anyway. But Gates was against it. He was going to leave Jamestown, such as it was, standing. And in order to make sure that at the last minute no one set it afire, he stayed on the riverbank until all two hundred and ten settlers were on board. Then as a farewell salute he had a company of men fire their muskets.

Of course the departing settlers were watched. Up and down the river, Indian lookouts stood behind trees, crouched in the grass, stationed at high points, watching the procession of boats wind toward the coast. Yah ha ha! This was the end of the English! As soon as the boats had disappeared, the lookouts would run to all the tribes, to all the villages, to all the chiefs, shouting out the good news. They would carry the news like a gift to old Powhatan. But as it turned out, the news changed before it could even be delivered.

The Indians probably saw the strange ship before the English did. It was preceded by a longboat with men rowing up the river while the settlers sailed down the river, but not until the first gray light of dawn on June 8 did they catch sight of each other. As soon as they were close enough for voices to carry, the settlers called to ask what ship the others were from.

The flagship *De La Warre,* out of London.

Captain Samuel Argall in command. Lord De La Warre on board, come to take over the government of Jamestown. Two other ships following.

New settlers?

One hundred and fifty.

Food?

Supplies for a year.

Of course Sir Thomas Gates and his people turned around and sailed back to Jamestown. Some of the old-timers may have hated to go back, but everyone agreed: this was God's doing. Had they left one tide earlier and had Lord De La Warre arrived one tide later, the ships would have missed each other. Like it or not, who could argue with God?

So the colony started over once again. The cannon was dug up, men retrieved their armor, and Lord De La Warre issued orders that everyone must work six hours a day. The church was to be repaired and supplied with wildflowers. Houses were to be rebuilt, fields planted, food gathered. Sir George Somers went to Bermuda to bring back wild hogs. (Unfortunately he ate so much pork in Bermuda that he died there.) Captain Samuel Argall went to Maine for fish. Later he went to the Potomac country, where the natives were willing to trade.

But Lord De La Warre did not make peace with neighboring Indians or with Powhatan. The killing went on: both sides killing, both sides taking revenge. Once the English murdered an Indian queen and all her children. Once Lord De La Warre had an Indian's hand cut off because he suspected the man of being a spy. When De La Warre sent messengers to Powhatan to ask for the weapons and captives stolen during the Starving Time, Powhatan refused to give up anything. Even for the sake of peace, he refused. Let the English get out of his country, he said. And if the governor wished to speak to him again, he should first send Powhatan a coach and three horses. That was how the English king traveled around, wasn't it?

Lord De La Warre was not happy in Jamestown. Not only did the Indians upset him, but he was sick. Hardly had he arrived when he came down with a violent case of malaria with a fever so high, blood was taken from him again and again, which only made him weaker. As soon as he had recovered from that, down he came with dysentery. Then gout. Then scurvy. Sometimes he was sick with all these ailments at once. He dragged himself around when he could, but after nine months no one could blame him for giving up and going back to London.

The settlers, who had been ruled by so many different men in so many different ways, must have wondered—what next?

Sir Thomas Dale, the new governor, blew into Jamestown on May 19, 1611, as if he were riding on the back of a storm cloud. He took one look at the settlement and decided that everything was wrong and that everyone was lazy. He was a harsh man who believed in harsh rules and strict obedience. The first time a man was caught swearing, for instance, he was whipped; the second time, he had a bodkin, a pointed instrument for making holes, thrust through his tongue; the third time, he was killed. If a man missed church three times without a good excuse, he had to serve six months as a galley slave. If he picked flowers or grapes without permission, he'd have his ears cut off. Two women settlers, who apparently sewed for the colony, were publicly whipped for making men's shirts too short. If John Smith believed in ruling by fear, Sir Thomas Dale believed in ruling by terror.

As for the Indians, Dale boasted that if England would send him two thousand convicts, he could wipe out the whole lot. He never got his convicts, but he made the most of the few hundred soldiers that he had. He didn't need a reason to attack the Indians. He just attacked. Sometimes in full armor. He had brought with him a lot of old armor from the Tower of London, and although a few Indians had seen armor before, never had they been attacked by a whole company of monsterlike men dressed in metal. When their arrows struck the metal and fell harmlessly to the ground, they were thrown into despair. How could they match such magic? They tried every chant, every spell, every charm they knew. They called on Okee to send rain to put out the burning wicks on the English muskets.

Still, neither the Indians nor the English gave up. Now Dale decided to spread the settlers up and down the river so there'd be no room left for Powhatan. He built four new forts and a new community eighty miles up the James River which the English named Henrico. Of course, while the English were actually building they could not wear armor, and this was when the Indians often attacked. Indeed, it was now that a minor Powhatan chief, Nemattanow, made himself famous. Covered with feathers which he plastered over his body and with a pair of swan's wings attached to his shoulders, Nemattanow told his people that his feathers were as strong magic as the English armor. No bullets could kill him, and, as it turned out, he did survive battle after battle. So Nemattanow became a hero to the Indians, proof that their gods were as strong as the English ones. The English called him Jack of the Feathers, and they went on building, expanding, and fighting.

By the spring of 1613 there were more than seven hundred settlers in Virginia (at least thirty were women), the town of Henrico was completed, and although a few Indian tribes had submitted to the English, Powhatan held firm.

As for Pocahontas, the English at Jamestown hadn't seen her for four years. She was seventeen years old now and may no longer have been living with her husband. Perhaps he had died or perhaps they had not been happy together. In any case, in April, 1613, she was alone in the Potomac country, staying at the home of the Potomac chief, when Samuel Argall arrived on a trading mission from Jamestown.

Quite accidentally Argall learned that Pocahontas was nearby, and he knew that he had stumbled on a prize, a chance at last to break Powhatan's will. All he had to do was kidnap Pocahontas and hold her as a hostage. Then Powhatan would give in fast enough. Then he'd return the weapons and captives that the settlers had been trying so hard and so long to get from him. Then he'd make peace.

Argall was too crafty a man to think he could go to Pocahontas and take her by force. No, she must be lured to his ship. She must walk on board of her own free will, not suspecting a trap had been laid for her until she was caught.

Argall sought his old friend Japizaws, brother of the

Potomac chief, and asked for help. Knowing how greedy Japizaws was for English goods, Argall showed him a handsome copper kettle which would be his if he got Pocahontas onto his ship.

Japizaws was willing to do anything for a kettle like that. His wife too.

So the next day they told Pocahontas that there was an English ship in the river. Wouldn't she like to go with them and take a look?

It had been a long time since Pocahontas had seen an English ship, yet she may have hesitated.

Just look?

Oh yes, just look.

Japizaws' wife was such a willful, loud-voiced woman, it would have been hard for Pocahontas to refuse her even if she had wanted to. In any case, she did go. And there was the ship, just like the ships at Jamestown. Its white wings were folded and tied to their tree trunks, the way they always were when ships were at rest.

But as soon as Japizaws' wife saw the ship, she was no longer content just to look. Oh no, she must go on board, she cried. She must see more. She and her husband had rehearsed what they would do, and they did it well. She wailed and begged. He scolded and refused to let her go. What was she thinking of? he asked. It would not be proper for one woman to go on a ship that held only men.

Still Japizaws' wife carried on, making such a fuss that Japizaws finally threw up his hands.

If she must go, he shouted, then let her go. But she must take Pocahontas so there would be two women together.

By this time Captain Argall had undoubtedly come ashore and invited the three of them to eat with him on his ship. But Pocahontas held back, knowing that her father wouldn't want her on an English ship, eating with an English captain.

But there was no end to the commotion that Japizaws' wife was raising. On and on. Nothing would do but that she must eat on the ship.

And at last Pocahontas gave in, perhaps simply out of embarrassment to keep her friend quiet. Of her own free will she walked into the trap that had been set for her, and, unsuspecting, she sat down at the captain's table. Of course she didn't know that all during the meal Japizaws was kicking Samuel Argall under the table. Sly little kicks. See? he seemed to be saying. She's here. Don't forget the kettle.

After eating, Pocahontas was taken to the gunner's room for a rest, and in her absence Japizaws and his wife were given their kettle. But Pocahontas couldn't rest. Once she was alone, she became more and more uneasy about what she'd done. She shouldn't be here. And she wouldn't stay, not a minute longer. She went on deck, but when she started to go ashore, she found her way blocked.

She was not going ashore, she was told. She was going to Jamestown.

No! She wouldn't go. She couldn't go. But she was surrounded. No matter which way she turned, the English were there to stop her.

She protested, she argued, she cried. According to the report of the man who kept the records for Jamestown, Japizaws and wife, pretending to have no part in the plot, cried right along with her. For a little while. Then "with the kettle and other toys, [they] went merrily on shore."

And Pocahontas went to Jamestown.

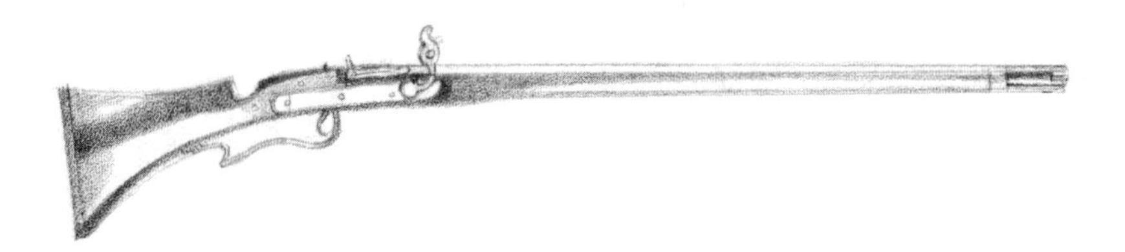

Pocahontas kept telling herself that she'd be a captive for only a short time. As soon as her father was told what had happened, he'd do whatever he had to do to free her. And as soon as Argall's ship reached Jamestown, messengers were sent to Powhatan telling him that in order to have his daughter back, he must give up his guns, send back the English captives, and agree to peace. Pocahontas knew these were hard terms, but at least they were terms. She wasn't a common captive without hope of release. So while she waited, she asked about John Smith. Only a few old-timers were left ("ancients," they called themselves), but whenever she met one, she asked. Every time she was told what the Indians were always told: John Smith was dead.

Pocahontas did not stay in Jamestown long. Sir Thomas Gates (back from England and governor again) and Sir Thomas Dale (now marshal of the colony) decided she should go upriver to live at Rock Hall, the one-hundred-acre parsonage across from Henrico. With five forts surrounding the area, Pocahontas would be better protected in case the Indians should try to recapture her. She would also receive the best religious instruction. The English had no intention of letting Pocahontas slip through their hands without trying to turn her into a Christian first. Twenty-six-year-old Reverend Alexander Whitaker at Rock Hall, they figured, was just the man for the job. Indeed, the only reason he had come to Virginia was because he believed it was more important to turn heathens into Christians than it was to turn people who were already Christians into better

Christians. Naturally he was pleased to have Pocahontas in his care; she was the only heathen he'd had a chance to work on.

But first she must be dressed so she would at least look like a Christian. So the ladies in Reverend Whitaker's church put Pocahontas into tight-waisted dresses with stiff, scratchy ruffs around the neck. They gave her long awkward petticoats to wear. And in place of her soft moccasins, they had her squeeze her feet into hard-soled leather shoes.

Everyone was nice to her. They told her she would get used to English clothes; she should just take smaller steps. When Pocahontas spoke of Okee, Mr. Whitaker explained gently that Okee was not a god but a devil. When he heard her singing her magic chants, he didn't scold; he just said that her magic was worthless. When she raised her arm to call on the Sun to be her witness, he said the sun could neither see nor hear. But she knew better. The Sun saw everything. Who but the Sun knew the truth so well? Mr. Whitaker talked and talked, not only privately to her but twice a day at church. There were new words—*sin, idols, heaven, hell,* but they may have simply drifted around her like falling leaves while she waited to go home.

Weeks went by. One month, then two. Sometimes at night when Pocahontas heard strange sounds in the woods beyond the parsonage, she would take hope. There! she would think. There were her father's warriors come to fight for her release.

But no warriors came.

Often she must have remembered the time her father sent her to seek the release of his men who had been captured. "Don't beg," Powhatan had told her. But he had sent relatives to beg; he had sent deer as a gift. He had tried every way to have those captives freed.

Once Opechancanough, who hated the English even more than Powhatan did, had humbled himself for the sake of his captives. He had thrown down his glove before the English as a sign of surrender. Of course he had felt shame, but he had done it.

But who was doing anything for her? Sometimes she could not help but think: If John Smith were alive, this would not have happened.

It was not until the end of the third month that Powhatan replied to the ransom demands. He wanted his daughter back, he said, but unfortunately his weapons had all been lost or stolen. He had only seven muskets left, and they were broken. Still, he sent them back, along with seven English captives. As soon as his daughter was returned, he'd give the English five hundred bushels of corn, he promised, and then he'd make peace.

Not for one minute did the English believe the story of the lost weapons.

Nor did Pocahontas. Seven broken muskets! Was that all she was worth? She knew her father loved his guns, but did he love them more than he did her? Had he not always said that she was as dear to him as his life? Was he so proud that he couldn't bend his knee even for her? Did he mean to let her stay here forever, always walking with small steps, speaking the sharp English speech like twigs snapping. Love you not me? Love you not me? How long had it been since she had heard her own people speak! Long, flowing talk, but rough like water running over pebbles.

Perhaps it was loneliness that finally drove Pocahontas to give Reverend Whitaker her attention. All her life she had lived close to sisters and brothers and aunts and uncles, believing what they did, doing everything together. Perhaps one day in church, looking at the people around her, she had thought, Well, I will become one of them. If her people didn't want her, if she was to live here forever, what else was she to do? In her long skirts, she may already have felt less like an Indian. In any case, she did begin to give in to the Christian words. Some of them were comforting, and certainly she needed comfort. Besides, they were the same words that John Smith believed. And one day she and John would meet in the Christian heaven that Mr. Whitaker talked about if she accepted his god. So she slowly moved from one world to another, but it was not only Mr. Whitaker whom she listened to. There was another man who helped her on her way.

His name was John Rolfe. A handsome twenty-eight-year-old widower, he was a survivor of the Bermuda shipwreck, and since joining the colony he had become best known for his interest in tobacco. Ever since tobacco had been brought to England from the West Indies in the late 1500s, smoking had become the fashion. King James hated it. He said smoking was ugly to look at, nasty to smell, bad for the brain and awful for the lungs, but in spite of the king, young men all over England were pulling on pipes, puffing, and blowing smoke rings. John Rolfe, a chain smoker, was determined not only to raise tobacco in Virginia but to raise enough of it so he could sell it to England. In 1613 he was experimenting with a high grade of West Indian tobacco which he had planted at or near Henrico.

John Rolfe and Pocahontas probably first met at church, but it was not long before he began dropping in at the parsonage, offering to help Pocahontas with English lessons, reading to her from the Bible. John was lonely, his wife having died soon after arriving in Jamestown, his baby daughter having died in Bermuda. But he was a serious-minded, proper, religious man whose best friend was Sir

Thomas Dale, and, like him, he believed in living by rules. So he was somewhat surprised when he found himself becoming interested not only in Pocahontas' religion but in Pocahontas herself. Perhaps he was falling in love, although Christian men were not supposed to fall in love with heathen women. It was even written in the Bible that God did not like men to take "strange" wives—women with different religions and different customs. John Rolfe carried on long arguments with himself, for he had to admit that Pocahontas was "strange." Her education (as he wrote) had been "rude, her manner barbarous, her generation accursed." So what was he to do?

Pocahontas, who of course was also lonely, knew exactly what to do. She studied hard. She learned to say the Lord's Prayer and to recite the Apostle's Creed. When Reverend Whitaker asked her the questions of the catechism, she was able to give the right answer to every one, whether she knew what it meant or not. In the spring of 1614 she said she was ready to become a Christian. At her baptism, she was required to renounce Okee, to declare that all her former beliefs were false and evil; hard as it may have been, she said what she was supposed to. Perhaps she was truly convinced. Perhaps with her new name, Rebecca, which the settlers gave her at her conversion, she willed herself away from her old world into her new one. At least as much as she could. For how could she completely part with the Indian in her? How could she ever take the Sun for granted in the careless way that the English did?

By this time John Rolfe had stopped arguing with himself. Indeed, he'd decided it was God's will that he should marry Pocahontas. (He had already found out that it was Pocahontas' will too.) In England people would surely be glad for the marriage, he reasoned. They had always preached conversion, and here was Powhatan's own daughter, a princess, not only converted but becoming English by marriage. John Rolfe listed all the reasons in favor of the marriage and wrote Sir Thomas Dale for permission to go ahead.

Dale thought the marriage was a splendid idea, but he didn't know how Powhatan would take it. First he thought he'd make one last try to get those guns. As usual, Dale's method was to fight for what he wanted, so in March, 1614, he took Pocahontas and one hundred and fifty men upriver, informing whatever natives he saw that the English wanted their guns back; if they didn't get them, they'd burn down the native villages, take their canoes, destroy their fishing nets. When the Indians responded by shooting arrows at the English, Dale did just what he had said he'd do.

And what did Pocahontas think of this? Probably she'd seen enough war in her life to accept that this was how men behaved, Indians and English alike, but by now she was convinced that no matter what Dale did, Powhatan was not going to part with those guns. Not for her sake or for the sake of peace.

Later two of Pocahontas' brothers came on the ship to see how she was. They could see that she'd been well treated, even though she looked strange in her English clothes. But she was certainly in a bad temper. She told them that as far as she was concerned, her father could keep his old guns. She had waited and waited. Almost a year she had waited to come home, but now she wasn't coming home at all. She was going to stay with the English and marry an Englishman. Let them tell her father that.

The English were back in Jamestown when Powhatan heard the news. It was not only his pride that had been at stake but his very kingship. Those guns (many of them won in war, taken from the dead) had become a symbol of power between him and the English, even among his own people. Surrender would be total surrender and he would never agree to that.

But now all that had changed. If Pocahontas was no longer a hostage, he had no need to surrender. He could offer; he could make the first move. Quickly he sent messengers to Dale. He was ready for peace, he said. If Pocahontas was to marry an Englishman, this was a sign of true friendship. He would even return some weapons. He wouldn't attend the wedding, since he had vowed never to step into an English settlement, but he would appoint one of his brothers to take his place. He sent Pocahontas a string of freshwater pearls as a wedding present, and several pieces of land.

On April 5, 1614, the wedding took place in the Jamestown church, with many of the settlers and some of Pocahontas' own family attending. Pocahontas wore a long dress made of the richest-looking material that could be found in Jamestown. With it she wore a muslin tunic, a white veil, and the string of pearls her father gave her. Reverend Buck, who had christened John Rolfe's baby girl in Bermuda and later buried her, performed the ceremony, and at the end of the service Pocahontas was not only officially married, she was officially English. It would have been strange if it did not occur to her that now she was a countryman of John Smith's, even if he was dead.

The settlers called the peace that followed the Peace of Pocahontas. Sir Thomas Dale was so impressed at the way one marriage had turned the Indians into friends, he didn't see why another marriage wouldn't make them even better friends. Powhatan had another daughter whom he now called his favorite. Why shouldn't Sir Thomas Dale himself marry her? It didn't seem to trouble him that he already had a wife in England. No, he went right ahead and sent Ralph Hamor, an officer of the colony, to see Powhatan and make arrangements.

The first thing that Powhatan wanted, however, was news of Pocahontas. How were his daughter and his new son-in-law getting along? he asked. And of course Ralph Hamor reported that Pocahontas was happy. So happy, he said, that she would never wish to return to her old home.

Powhatan laughed as if Hamor had made a joke. When had Pocahontas ever been given a chance to go home? But when Ralph Hamor mentoned a second daughter for Sir Thomas Dale, Powhatan said No. That daughter was already promised to a chief; besides, one daughter was enough for the English. But to show that he was still Dale's friend, he sent him some animal skins. In return he wanted a shaving knife, a grindstone, two bone combs, one hundred fishhooks, a cat, and a dog.

In London, people were delighted to hear of the conversion of Pocahontas, then of her marriage, then of the birth of her son, Thomas, a year later. But now that there was peace, they asked, why didn't more Indians become Christians? Now that there was peace, why weren't the settlers making money? They seemed to have failed at everything they tried. They couldn't grow pineapples or oranges or raise silkworms or make wine even though they'd been sent grapes from France. They had trouble even feeding themselves. Eventually John Rolfe's tobacco would turn out to be their big money-maker, but they didn't know this yet. At the moment Londoners were so sick of Virginia and its problems that they were giving their money and their attention to their new colony in Bermuda.

Then Sir Thomas Dale had a grand idea for reviving interest in Virginia. In the spring of 1616 he was going to England, so why not take Pocahontas and John Rolfe and little Thomas to England with him? The Virginia backers would have a real, live Indian princess to show off. She'd go to parties with lords and ladies. She'd meet the king and queen. She'd go to church and pray English prayers along with English people. The English might look down on Indians as "savages," but they were crazy about the idea of "royal savages," and Bermuda didn't have a single royal savage to its name. (In fact, it had no Indians at all.)

Of course Pocahontas would have to travel in style like any princess. So in April, 1616, when Dale's party set sail, Pocahontas was accompanied by ten or twelve Indians in addition to her sister Matachanna, who was to serve as nurse for little Thomas. Powhatan sent a special ambassador along—Tomocomo, a hardheaded man who would not likely be taken in by the splendors of England as Namontack had been. Powhatan wanted more than fancy stories about chariots and stone towers this time. How many people were there in England? He gave Tomocomo a stick so he could make notches and keep track of the number. Powhatan also wanted to know more about the king and queen. And about the English god. What did he look like? And Tomocomo was to ask about John Smith. Was he really dead or not?

5

No matter how much Namontack had told the Indians about London, they could never have imagined what it was really like. Not even Pocahontas could have been prepared for this gigantic, boisterous, noisy, crowded city: horses, carriages, and carts fighting each other for room on the narrow streets; people shouting that they had scissors for sale, hot buns for sale, flowers for sale. Buy here, buy here, buy, buy, buy, they cried. Even buildings seemed to be in competition—pushing against each other, rooftops rising over other rooftops, windows staring down other windows as if to make sure no one was getting ahead of anyone else. Even church bells clanged for attention—crossly, it seemed, each bell trying to drown out the others. Undoubtedly John Rolfe had described the famous London Bridge, but Pocahontas wouldn't have expected the business of the city to continue without letup right over the water. Stores, houses, buildings packed together on the bridge itself. Perhaps the only things in all of London that might even faintly have reminded Pocahontas of her girlhood home were the poles at the end of the bridge. They had human heads on top of them. Heads that had been cut off enemies or criminals.

Yet nothing in England affected Pocahontas as much as the news she heard on her first arrival. John Smith was alive. Indeed, he was in London.

Right now?

Right now. He had recently returned from exploring

New England, she was told, and he was hoping to go back. But he was here now.

If Pocahontas had ever been unhappy about coming to London, she was unhappy no longer. Secretly her heart must have turned cartwheels. Here they were countrymen, both in the same country at the same time! He'd be calling on her any day. Any minute.

He must have known that she was there. Everyone in London seemed to know. She couldn't step out of the inn where the Rolfes were staying without people on the street stopping to gawk. She couldn't attend a party without the news circulating through town. Yet John did not call. She looked for him on the streets, at parties, but she didn't see him.

Lady De La Warre took charge of Pocahontas, seeing that she had the proper clothes, instructing her in formal manners, introducing her to lords and ladies, preparing her for her presentation to the king and queen. And Pocahontas did well. Wherever she went, Londoners remarked on her regal bearing and her correct behavior. Yet Pocahontas could not help but notice that the strangers who met her always seemed surprised and the Virginia backer who introduced her always acted proud. It was if the Virginia people were saying, "See? She is an example of how well we can civilize savages." And as if the strangers were replying, "Well, we must civilize them all." She would have heard snatches of plans that were being proposed: a school for Indian children in Henrico; a campaign to eliminate heathen priests. When people praised Pocahontas for having brought peace to Virginia, there was something about their praise that suggested she should be able to keep peace in Virgina. When they discussed their plans for her people, it was as if she had a share in carrying them out. Obviously they believed that their plans were truly *for* her people and not against them, yet she knew these plans would lead to trouble.

If only she could talk to John Smith! But he didn't come.

Meanwhile Pocahontas was entertained by the Bishop of London. At Christmas she attended the court's Christmas festival, sitting on the special platform with the royal party. An engraving made of her at this time shows the face of a strong-minded woman surrounded by a high lace collar. Although she looks severe and older than her years, her mouth shows a hint of merriment as if it were something remembered from long ago.

Indeed, there was not much reason to be merry now. Perhaps her happiest times came when she could be alone with Matachanna and little Thomas. Now she could take off her hard-soled shoes and her scratchy ruffs, relax into her native language, and allow her old self to speak out. Best of all, she could in Indian style share her pleasure in little Thomas, who had become so important in her life.

There is no record of what Pocahontas thought of London and her social life. Perhaps she shared her impressions only with Matachanna; perhaps not even with her. But it is clear what Tomocomo thought. He had no use for the English at all. Of course he had to admit that there were a lot of them—more than there were leaves on the trees, he said. Far too many to count. (He had thrown away his stick at the first sight of England.) But numbers were all they had. Their streets smelled; their river was dirty, their air was unfit to breathe; pickpockets roamed the city; and crazy people were locked away in special buildings, while of course Indians knew that crazy people were the ones whom the gods most often spoke through.

Dressed in Indian fashion, painted and feathered as usual, Tomocomo even argued about religion with the Bishop of London. With Sir Thomas Dale acting as interpreter, he asked the Bishop what the English god looked like, but the Bishop couldn't even show him a picture. A lot of fair-sounding words he gave, but none of them added up to arms or legs or even a head. A poor sort of god, Tomocomo reasoned. One who didn't even tell the men how to wear their hair. Indian men all wore their hair the same way: long on the left side, shaved close on the right so it wouldn't interfere with their bowstrings. And how did they know to do this? Because Okee told them. Just as He told them how to grow corn, something else the English god knew nothing about.

But what about their king? Tomocomo asked. When was he going to see him?

He had already met the king, he was told, but Tomocomo denied this. When the occasion was described, however, Tomocomo was shocked. That puny little man was the *king?* That man who walked with a shuffle? If that was the king, he was a stingy, mean sort of king, Tomocomo declared. The English gave Powhatan a white dog which Powhatan loved so much, he fed him from his own plate. But the English king gave Tomocomo nothing. "And I am better than your white dog," he said.

Moreover, the English were liars and deceivers. Look at how they had lied about John Smith! And look at how John Smith himself was behaving! He had accepted the friendship of Pocahontas in her country, yet in his country did he offer his friendship in return? Had he called yet?

No, he had not called.

Of course Pocahontas did not know that on her arrival

John Smith had written a long letter to Queen Anne, praising Pocahontas, listing all the ways she had been a friend to Jamestown, and recommending her to the queen's special attention. John was pleased to write the letter, not only for the sake of Pocahontas but because it gave him a chance to remind the queen what a big part he'd played in the founding of Jamestown. Indeed, he wanted so desperately to get back to the New World, he was retelling his adventures to anyone who might help him. John was not a man who gave his heart to people, either men or women (he never married); he was not interested in games or sports or society as so many men were. He had only one passion: America. And his mind was on America now, not Pocahontas, although he knew that out of simple courtesy he should see her. Yet he may have dreaded the meeting. Suppose she had not outgrown that childish notion of their special kinship? It was one thing to play the part of a brother to a little girl, but to a married woman? Well, it would be awkward. For whatever reasons, John Smith was in no hurry to make this call.

Disappointed again and again, Pocahontas gradually gave up hoping, especially after the Rolfes moved into the country, away from London's polluted air that was bothering all the Indians.

Pocahontas felt more at home in the country house surrounded by trees. She could be happy here with little Thomas, and she begged John Rolfe to let them all stay. But John always said No. He had been made secretary of the colony, and he was proud of his appointment and anxious to return to his tobacco fields. Pocahontas was afraid to go back to Jamestown. Yet how could she explain her fears to this man who had lived with her three years and had never tried to understand the Indian in her? He spoke of how easy it would be to turn thousands of her people ("poore, wretched and mysbelieving people," he called them) into Christians. He might expect her to help. Indeed, the English were full of plans for putting converted Indians to work at converting their own people. Didn't the English see how painful, even impossible, this would be? No, they understood nothing, it seemed. John even said that the Indians would be very willing to part with their children so they could be educated to English ways, but of course Pocahontas knew better. As true a Christian as she may have become, she knew that her people valued their religion as staunchly as the English valued theirs. Perhaps she didn't even like to think of a time when no one would greet the Sun from the river, when no one would dance around the sacred fire.

More than ever, Pocahontas must have been troubled by the double nature of her life. On the one hand, there was her husband, determined to take the very "Indian-ness" out of her people, whom he called "barbarous" and "wretched." On the other hand, there was Tomocomo, disdaining everything English, determined to set her father against them. In Jamestown conflict would surely break out. And she would be caught in the middle. Young Thomas too. Oh, let them stay in England, she prayed.

The first three months of the winter of 1617 were warm but damp and very windy. Pocahontas found the dampness bad for her health. Not used to the English climate or to English diseases, Indians in England often developed tuberculosis or other chest problems. Two of Pocahontas' party died that winter, and even in the country Pocahontas coughed and felt more and more tired. Still, she did welcome the wind. No ship could sail to America in such a strong wind, so the longer and the harder the wind blew, the better Pocahontas liked it.

On one of those damp, windy days at the end of February or the first part of March, John Smith decided that he wouldn't put off his call on Pocahontas any longer. He took several friends with him, perhaps to ease his sense of awkwardness, and made the nine-mile trip up the Thames River to the house where the Rolfes were staying. Pocahontas of course had no warning of the visit. Apparently she went to the door herself, and when she saw John Smith standing so casually as if he were any visitor, as if it didn't matter when he came, her first reaction was anger. She greeted him coldly, but then memory swept over her in such a sudden storm of feeling, she put her hands over her face and turned away. Both John Smith and John Rolfe, who had joined them, tried to smooth things over and jolly her into normal conversation, but nothing they said made any difference. Pocahontas wouldn't talk. Indeed, she couldn't. At last John Rolfe suggested that the men take a walk while she composed herself.

It took Pocahontas several hours to recover, but when at last she spoke to John Smith, she was at no loss for words. Her speech was as if she had prepared it; her emotions she knew by heart. She stood as Powhatan's daughter, straight and proud, and reminded John of all she had done for him and his people. How could he have neglected her so? she asked. Did he even know that she had mourned him for years?

"They did tell us always you were dead," she said, "and I knew no other till I came to Plimouth."

She went on.

"You did promise Powhatan what was yours should bee his, and the like to you; you called him father, being in his land a stranger, and by the same reason so must I doe you."

John Smith was embarrassed. To cover his confusion before his friends, he explained that the term "father" applied to men of rank, a chief in his country, and he was not that. Moreover, Pocahontas was a princess, so it was not fitting for her to say "father."

Pocahontas set her face stubbornly. John Smith was not going to slip out of their special kinship so easily.

When John came to her father's country, she pointed out, he had made her father and all his people afraid. Everyone but her. What had happened to him that in his own country he should cringe at the use of a name?

She taunted him. "Feare you here I should call you father?" she asked.

"I tell you then I will," she declared, "and I will bee forever and ever your countrieman."

Forever and ever his countryman. Whether he liked it or not, that was what she was. That was the way she had willed it.

In his own account John Smith says no more about their meeting, but when he left, Pocahontas knew she would never see him again. Yet even now she would not entirely give up hope that she could stay in England. She prayed that something would intervene and keep them from going. She prayed that John Rolfe would change his mind. Every day she coughed more and became weaker, but either John did not notice or would not let himself be concerned.

Pocahontas was both an emotional woman and a strong one, as is evident in the account John Smith left of their meeting. And as the Sun or God (or both) would be her witness, she did not want to leave England. Yet in the end, no matter how strong, she was a woman and a wife. And the day that the wind dropped and her husband said they would sail, she did what was expected. Along with young Thomas, Matachanna, and Tomocomo, she went to London, where Sir Samuel Argall's ship, the *George,* lay waiting. Reluctantly but of her own free will she walked back into the same trap that she had walked into on the Potomac River. Only this time she recognized it for what it was. Indeed, had she ever really been free of it?

Pocahontas was taken to her sleeping quarters, too sick to take a last look at London's skyline as the *George* set sail. Too sick to welcome the daffodils standing at attention here and there in the countryside. Too sick to acknowledge her secret sisterhood to apple trees bursting into blossom along the riverbank.

Indeed, the *George* had gone only twenty-five miles down the Thames River, not even to the open sea, when Pocahontas knew she was just too sick to live. At the little town of Gravesend she begged to be taken ashore, and even John Rolfe could see now that she was in a serious state. So the *George* dropped anchor, and Pocahontas was taken to a nearby inn. A doctor was called, but it was too late for anyone to help. At the age of twenty-one Pocahontas died and was buried in the country she had lived in less than a year but had not wanted to leave. People reported that she died like a Christian. She also died like an Indian, showing no fear of death. She told John not to grieve. "All men must die," she said. The important thing was that their son, two-year-old Thomas, lived.

And at least Thomas did not go back to America. After a hurried funeral service, Thomas, who was not well, was left in the care of John Rolfe's brother, Henry. He did not go back to Virginia until he was twenty years old, and of course by that time he was thoroughly English. Perhaps his only feeling for the Indian in him came from the many stories he must have heard about his mother while he was growing up. It would be nice to think that sometime during these years he met John Smith and that John told him about the little girl who turned cartwheels in Jamestown.

Epilogue

Pocahontas was right to have worried that the English would go too far in trying to make over her people. As it turned out, the Indians had not been willing to give up their children; the school at Henrico had not worked out; very little converting took place. But in 1619 (one year after the death of Powhatan) George Thorpe arrived in the colony, and he had ideas for converting that in a sense were meant to break the Indians. His theory was that the Indians would forget their own gods and their heathen practices if the English were only kind enough, if the English gave them what they wanted, if the English would get them so used to English life that they wouldn't want to live any other way. So when the Indians complained that they were afraid of the colony's mastiff dogs, Thorpe had some of the dogs shot in their presence. For Opechancanough, who had replaced Powhatan as chief, he had an English house built that was supposed to make him a friend for life. And indeed Opechancanough was pleased, especially with the front door that had a lock on it. He kept going in and out, in and out, turning the key and marveling. Thorpe taught the Indians to use guns, invited them to eat with the English and sleep in their homes whenever they wished.

All this was hard on the Indians in exactly the way Thorpe had meant it to be. When the Indians had fought the English, they had had no trouble holding on to their pride, nor when they had simply traded with the English in peace. But where was their pride now? Many of the Indians sensed that Thorpe's system was an underhanded way of luring them away from their own customs, their group feeling, their beliefs. Opechancanough, however, had his own underhanded scheme. He encouraged his people to be friendly to the English, to mingle with them freely, to lull them into feeling safe. As part of his campaign, Opechancanough told Thorpe that he had decided that the English god was really better than the Indian one. Furthermore, he told the English they could settle anywhere on the rivers that they wanted, as long as there were no Indians already there. All Opechancanough had to do now was wait for the right moment to strike.

That moment came in March, 1622, when the much-loved Indian hero, Jack of the Feathers, was shot by a couple of English servants. Knowing that he was dying, Jack begged the servants not to tell his people. Bury him with the English, he said, so no one would know that, in spite of his boasting, an English bullet had killed him. But the Indians did find out, and as soon as Opechancanough heard about it he set the time for his long-planned all-out attack. Eight o'clock on Friday morning, March 22.

The Indians kept their secret well, making light of their hero's death, helping the English with their work just as usual, visiting, acting so normal that on Friday morning when groups of Indians called at farmhouses throughout the colony, the English had no reason to suspect that anything was wrong. It was a massive, well-timed move. At the end of the day more than one-fourth of the English colony, about three hundred and fifty men, women, and children, had been killed. George Thorpe had not only been killed, he had been butchered.

As it happened, John Rolfe (who had remarried an Englishwoman) barely escaped the attack. He had died of natural causes only a few days before.

As soon as John Smith heard about the terrible uprising, he wrote a plan for reviving the colony and offered to carry out the plan himself. But his plan was rejected and no one offered to send him back to Virginia. Nor did he ever become a member of the New England settlement that he had so much wanted to join. He spent his last years writing about the New World and feeling that, as one of the first adventurers, he deserved more recognition and financial reward than he had received. He died in London on June 21, 1631, at the age of fifty-one.

As for the Virginia colony, of course it did survive, and in time it prospered, simply because, as Tomocomo had noted, England had so many people. And more and more of those people came to Virginia when they saw how well tobacco grew there and how much money it brought. In the long run the Indians didn't stand a chance. They were pushed back and pushed back until no room was left for them.

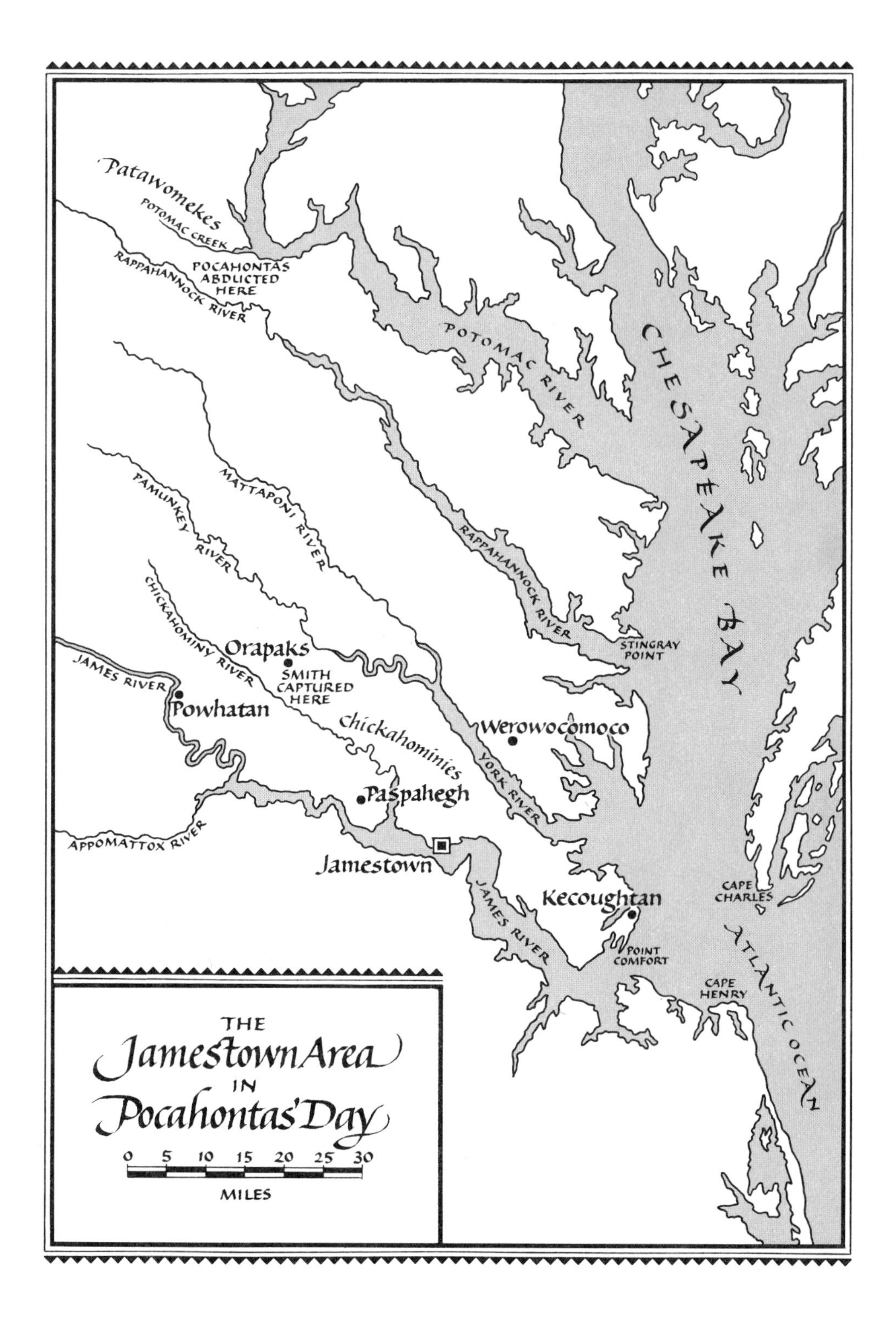

Patawomekes
POTOMAC CREEK
POCAHONTAS ABDUCTED HERE
RAPPAHANNOCK RIVER
POTOMAC RIVER
CHESAPEAKE BAY
MATTAPONI RIVER
PAMUNKEY RIVER
RAPPAHANNOCK RIVER
STINGRAY POINT
CHICKAHOMINY RIVER
Orapaks
SMITH CAPTURED HERE
JAMES RIVER
Powhatan
Chickahominies
Werowocomoco
YORK RIVER
Paspahegh
APPOMATTOX RIVER
Jamestown
Kecoughtan
JAMES RIVER
POINT COMFORT
CAPE CHARLES
CAPE HENRY
ATLANTIC OCEAN
THE Jamestown Area IN Pocahontas' Day
0 5 10 15 20 25 30
MILES

Notes

Page 9. No one is sure of Pocahontas' exact age, but it is generally agreed that she was between ten and thirteen in 1607. Since she is supposed to have been twenty-one when she died in 1617, I have made her eleven.

All the Indians in the Powhatan confederacy were Algonquians. Powhatan had inherited six tribes and conquered twenty-five more tribes shortly before the English came in 1607. Each tribe had its own chief, but all were subject to Powhatan. The total population was about nine thousand. Powhatan's kingdom went up the Potomac River, west to the present site of Richmond, and south to the vicinity of the North Carolina border.

Page 10. Before Queen Isabella of Spain agreed to finance Columbus' expedition, King Henry VII of England was asked to do it but wasn't interested. Naturally the English later regretted that they had turned down this chance to reach the New World first.

Right through the seventeenth and eighteenth centuries men kept looking for a northern route by water that would be a shortcut to the Pacific Ocean. Not until the early twentieth century did Roald Amundsen find such a route, but it was through the Arctic and not such a shortcut after all.

Page 11. The settlers were also instructed to try to find the "Lost Colony" of Roanoke, North Carolina. Settled in 1587, the colony had completely disappeared when the English came back with supplies in 1591. No members of the Lost Colony were found, but there is a theory that they had moved north toward Chesapeake Bay and the few remaining members were murdered by Powhatan's people about the time of John Smith's arrival.

The trip from England took so long because the ships were kept by contrary winds for six weeks within sight of England before they could get under way.

Page 13. John may have learned some native language from captured Indians in London. He seems to have learned quickly, but in the meantime the English and the Indians found they could communicate fairly well in sign language. Later they exchanged young men for the express purpose of learning each other's language and becoming interpreters.

Page 16. The garter John Smith wore was just a band of cloth buckled below the knee to keep his stockings up.

Page 17. The magic disk was, of course, a compass.

Page 20. John Smith showed Rawhunt and the guards how the cannon worked. He had one cannon filled with stones and shot it at a tree which was weighted down with ice. The crashing branches, the cascading ice, and the tremendous roar impressed the natives more than ever.

Archer and Ratcliffe were planning to steal a boat and run away to England.

Page 30. In London Namontack was passed off as Powhatan's son. He was told to keep his hat on in the presence of King James to show that they were equals.

Page 33. Stingray Point is at the mouth of the Rappahannock River.

Page 34. The falls in the James River are just below the present site of Richmond, Virginia.

Page 39. Newport also took a flying squirrel and an opossum back to King James.

John Smith called the gentlemen who were not used to work "tuftaffaty" men, men who liked to dress in silks and taffetas. The word had come to mean just "silly."

Page 40. "Dutchmen" was the term used by Smith, but it had a wider meaning at that time and probably referred to either German or Swiss. In any case, the "Dutchmen" did manage to trick the settlement into giving them swords, guns, powder, shot and pikes which they gave to Powhatan. Later Powhatan had the "Dutchmen" killed. If they had betrayed the English, he said, they might betray him as well.

Page 44. For safety's sake, Gates, Somers, and Newport should not have been on the same ship, but they couldn't agree on who should be on the flagship, so they all went.

Page 46. On the way back to England John Smith's ship came close to the ship of his friend Henry Hudson, but they did not see each other. Later the crew of Hudson's ship reported that the ship's cat had acted strangely, running back and forth and crying, just at the time that John Smith's ship was nearby.

Page 52. The Jamestown ships were not considered strong enough to cross the open sea. Gates planned to take the settlers up the coast to Newfoundland, where at this time of year there were many English fishing boats. The settlers would go back to England with the fishermen.

Page 54. Drawing blood from patients was considered a cure at this time for almost any disease. It was, of course, almost the worst thing that could be done.

Page 55. Henrico was named after King James's son Prince Henry.

Page 64. Indians in Virginia grew and smoked tobacco, but the English found their tobacco bitter. It was the West Indian variety that sold so well in England.

John Rolfe and his first wife named their baby Bermuda. Another woman who gave birth to a boy on the island named him Bermudas.

Page 65. Pocahontas would not have found it strange to be given a new name at her conversion. Her people often took new names when they made big changes in their lives. Opechancanough took the name Mangopeesomon in 1621 when he decided he was going to try to wipe out the English.

Reverend Whitaker chose the name Rebecca from the Bible because it was Rebecca's marriage to Isaac which united two different peoples. The English hoped that Pocahontas' conversion would also unite two peoples.

Page 66. Sir Thomas Dale was acting as governor again while Gates was in England.

Page 74. Since John Rolfe had no royal blood and was not even an ambassador to a king, he was not invited to any of the court functions. Pocahontas and Tomocomo left him at home.

Page 78. Two young women in Pocahontas' party were sent to Bermuda to become Christians and to find English husbands. It was hoped that they would then go to Jamestown and work at converting the Indians there. No further record of this has been found.

Page 79. The ship that carried the Rolfes to England docked first at Plymouth before proceeding to London.

Page 84. More English would have been killed, but at the last minute a friendly Indian (who had turned Christian) warned them and they were able to defend themselves or get away.

Bibliography

Andrews, K. R. "Christopher Newport of Limehouse, Mariner," *William & Mary Quarterly,* 3rd Series, 1954, 28–41.

Arber, Edward, ed. *Travels and Works of John Smith.* Edinburgh: John Grant, 1910.

Barbour, Philip L., ed. *The Jamestown Voyages under the First Charter, 1606–1609.* Cambridge, England: Cambridge University Press, 1969.

———. *Pocahontas and Her World.* Boston: Houghton Mifflin, 1970.

———. *The Three Worlds of John Smith.* Boston: Houghton Mifflin, 1964.

Berkhofer, Robert F., Jr. *The White Man's Indian.* New York: Random House, 1978.

Beverly, Robert T. *The History and Present State of Virginia.* Chapel Hill: University of North Carolina Press, 1947.

Billings, Warren M., ed. *The Old Dominion in the Seventeenth Century.* Chapel Hill: University of North Carolina Press, 1975.

Birch, Thomas. *The Court and Times of James the First.* London: Henry Colburn, 1848.

Bradley, A. G. *Captain John Smith.* New York: Macmillan, 1905.

Bridenbaugh, Carl. *Early Americans.* New York: Oxford University Press, 1981.

———. *Jamestown, New York.* New York: Oxford University Press, 1980.

Brown, Alexander. *The Genesis of the United States.* Boston: Houghton Mifflin, 1890.

Chamberlain, John. *The Chamberlain Letters,* ed. Elizabeth Thomson. New York: G. P. Putnam's Sons, 1965.

Chatterton, E. Keble. *Captain John Smith.* London: John Lane, 1927.

Craven, Wesley Frank. *The Southern Colonies in the Seventeenth Century, 1607–1689.* Baton Rouge: Louisiana State University Press, 1949.

Fausz, John Frederick. *The Powhatan Uprising of 1622: A Historical Study of Ethnocentrism and Cultural Conflict.* Ph.D. dissertation. Williamsburg: College of William and Mary, 1977.

Forbes, Jack D. *The Indian in America's Past.* Englewood Cliffs: Prentice-Hall, 1964.

Garnett, David. *Pocahontas.* New York: Harcourt Brace, 1933.
Hamor, Ralph. *The True Discourse of the Present Estate of Virginia, June, 1614.* London, 1615. (Facsimile edition, n.d.)
Hariot, Thomas. *A Briefe and True Report of the New Found Land of Virginia, 1588.* Ann Arbor: University of Michigan microfilm.
Hartzog, Henry S. *John Smith and Pocahontas.* St. Louis: D'Alroy & Hart, 1937.
Highwater, Jamake. *The Primal Mind.* New York: Harper and Row, 1981.
Hume, Ivor Noel. *Here Lies Virginia.* New York: Knopf, 1963.
———. *Martin's Hundred.* New York: Knopf, 1982.
Jennings, Francis. *The Invasion of America.* New York: Norton, 1975.
Johnson, F. Roy. *The Algonquins.* Murfreesboro, N.C.: Johnson Publishing Co., 1972.
Lee, Dorothy. *Freedom and Culture.* Englewood Cliffs: Prentice-Hall, 1959.
Lewis, Clifford M., and Albert J. Loomie. *The Spanish Jesuit Mission, 1570–72.* Chapel Hill: University of North Carolina Press, 1953.
McCary, Ben C. *Indians in the Seventeenth Century.* Jamestown Booklet No. 31. Charlottesville: University of Virginia Press, 1957.
McElwee, William. *The Wisest Fool in Christendom.* New York: Harcourt Brace, 1958.
Morgan, Edmund S. *American Slavery—American Freedom.* New York: Norton, 1975.
Morton, Richard L. *Colonial Virginia.* Chapel Hill: University of North Carolina Press, 1960.
Mossiker, Frances. *Pocahontas.* New York: Knopf, 1976.
Nash, Gary B. *Red, White, and Black.* Englewood Cliffs: Prentice-Hall, 1982.
Porter, Henry Culverwell. "Alexander Whitaker: Cambridge Apostle to Virginia," *William & Mary Quarterly,* 3rd Series, XIV (1959), pp. 317–343.
Quinn, David Beers. *England and the Discovery of America, 1481–1620.* New York, Knopf, 1974.
Quinn, Vernon. *The Exciting Adventures of Captain John Smith.* New York: Frederick Stokes, 1928.
Rolfe, John. *A True Relation of the State of Virginia lefte by Sir Thomas Dale Knight in May last 1616.* New Haven: Yale University Press, 1951.
Sackville, Lionel. "Lord Sackville's Papers Respecting Virginia," *American Historical Review,* XXVII (1922), pp. 493–738.

Sheehan, B. *Savagism and Civility.* Cambridge: Cambridge University Press, 1980.
Simms, W. Gilmore. *The Life of Captain John Smith.* Boston: John Philbrick, 1854.
Smith, Bradford. *Captain John Smith.* New York: Lippincott, 1953.
Stith, William. *The History of the First Discovery and Settlement of Virginia.* New York and London: Johnson Reprint Corp., 1969.
Strachey, William. *Lawes Divine, Morale and Martiall, etc.,* ed. David H. Flaherty. Charlottesville: University of Virginia Press, 1969.
Tyler, Lyon Gardiner, ed. *Narratives of Early Virginia, 1606–1625.* New York: Scribner's, 1907.
Vaughan, Alden T. *American Genesis: Captain John Smith and the Founding of Virginia.* Boston: Little, Brown, 1975.
Wharton, Henry. *The Life of John Smith, English Soldier.* Chapel Hill: University of North Carolina Press, 1957.
Whitaker, Alexander. *Good Newes from Virginia.* London, 1613.
Woodward, Grace Steele. *Pocahontas.* Norman: University of Oklahoma Press, 1969.
Wright, J. Leitch. *The Only Land They Knew.* New York: Macmillan, 1981.

Index